SOME SHORT STORIES OF H.G.WELLS

INCLUDING THE INVASION OF MARS

AND

THE VALLEY OF THE SPIDERS

BY

H.G. WELLS

British Library Cataloguing-in-Publication Data
A catalogue record for this book is available from the
British Library

CONTENTS

H. G. WELLS

Herbert George Wells was born in Bromley, England in 1866. He apprenticed as a draper before becoming a pupil-teacher at Midhurst Grammar School in West Sussex. Some years later, Wells won a scholarship to the School of Science in London, where he developed a strong interest in biology and evolution, founding and editing the *Science Schools Journal*. However, he left before graduating to return to teaching, and began to focus increasingly on writing. His first major essay on science, 'The Rediscovery of the Unique', appeared in 1891. However, it was in 1895 that Wells seriously established himself as a writer, with the publication of the now iconic novel, *The Time Machine*.

Wells followed *The Time Machine* with the equally well-received *War of the Worlds* (1898), which proved highly popular in the USA, and was serialized in the magazine *Cosmopolitan*. Around the turn of the century, he also began to write extensively on politics, technology and the future, producing works *The Discovery of the Future* (1902) and *Mankind in the Making* (1903). An active socialist, in 1904 Wells joined the Fabian Society, and his 1905 book *A Modern Utopia* presented a vision of a socialist society founded on reason and compassion. Wells also penned a range of successful comic novels, such as *Kipps* (1905) and *The History of Mr Polly* (1910).

Wells' 1920 work, *The Outline of History*, was penned in response to the Russian Revolution, and declared that world would be improved by education, rather than revolution. It made Wells one of the most important political thinkers of the twenties and thirties, and he began to write for a number of journals and newspapers, even travelling to Russia to lecture Lenin and Trotsky on social reform. Appalled by the carnage of World War II, Wells began to work on a project dealing with the perils of nuclear war, but died before completing it. He is now regarded as one of the greatest science-fiction writers of all time, and an important political thinker.

THE MAGIC SHOP

H.G. WELLS

I had seen the Magic Shop from afar several times; I had passed it once or twice, a shop window of alluring little objects, magic balls, magic hens, wonderful cones, ventriloquist dolls, the material of the basket trick, packs of cards that *looked* all right, and all that sort of thing, but never had I thought of going in until one day, almost without warning, Gip hauled me by my finger right up to the window, and so conducted himself that there was nothing for it but to take him in. I had not thought the place was there, to tell the truth – a modest-sized frontage in Regent Street, between the picture shop and the place where the chicks run about just out of patent incubators – but there it was sure enough. I had fancied it was down nearer the Circus, or around the corner in Oxford Street, or even in Holborn; always over the way and a little inaccessible it had been, with something of the mirage in its position; but here it was now quite indisputably, and the fat end of Gip's pointing finger made a noise upon the glass.

'If I was rich,' said Gip, dabbing a finger at the Disappearing Egg, 'I'd buy myself that. And that' – which was The Crying Baby, Very Human – 'and that,' which was a mystery, and called, so a neat card asserted, 'Buy One and Astonish Your Friends.'

'Anything,' said Gip, 'will disappear under one of those cones. I have read about it in a book.

'And there, Dad, is the Vanishing Halfpenny – only they've put it this way up so's we can't see how it's done.'

Gip, dear boy, inherits his mother's breeding, and he did not propose to enter the shop or worry in any way; only, you know, quite unconsciously he lugged my finger doorward, and he made his interest clear.

'That,' he said, and pointed to the Magic Bottle.

'If you had that?' I said; at which promising inquiry he looked up with a sudden radiance.

'I could show it to Jessie,' he said, thoughtful as ever of others.

'It's less than a hundred days to your birthday, Gibbles,' I said, and laid my hand on the door-handle.

Gip made no answer, but his grip tightened on my finger, and so we came into the shop.

It was no common shop this; it was a magic shop and all the prancing precedence Gip would have taken in the matter of mere toys was wanting. He left the burden of the conversation to me.

It was a little, narrow shop, not very well lit, and the doorbell pinged again with a plaintive note as we closed it behind us. For a moment or so we were alone and could glance about us. There was a tiger in *papier-mâché* on the glass case that covered the low counter – a grave, kind-eyed tiger that waggled his head in a methodical manner; there were several crystal spheres, a china hand holding magic cards, a stock of magic fish-bowls in various sizes, and an immodest magic hat that shamelessly displayed its springs. On the floor were magic mirrors; one to draw you out long and thin, one to swell your head and vanish your legs, and one to make you short and fat like a draught; and while we were laughing at these the shopman, as I suppose, came in.

At any rate, there he was behind the counter – a curious, sallow, dark man, with one ear larger than the other and a chin like the toe-cap of a boot.

'What can we have the pleasure?' he said, spreading his long, magic fingers on the glass case; and so with a start we were aware of him.

'I want,' I said, 'to buy my little boy a few simple tricks.'

'Legerdemain?' he asked. 'Mechanical? Domestic?'

'Anything amusing?' said I.

'Um!' said the shopman, and scratched his head for a moment as if thinking. Then, quite distinctly, he drew from his head a glass ball. 'Something in this way?' he said, and held it out.

The action was unexpected. I had seen the trick done at entertainments endless times before – it's part of the common stock of conjurers – but I had not expected it here. 'That's good,' I said, with a laugh.

'Isn't it?' said the shopman.

Gip stretched out his disengaged hand to take this object and found merely a blank palm.

'It's in your pocket,' said the shopman, and there it was!

'How much will that be?' I asked.

'We make no charge for glass balls,' said the shopman, politely. 'We get them' – he picked one out of his elbow as he spoke – 'free.' He produced another from the back of his neck, and laid it beside its predecessor on the counter. Gip regarded his glass ball sagely, then directed a look of inquiry at the two on the counter, and finally brought his round-eyed scrutiny to the shopman, who smiled. 'You may have those, too,' said the shopman, 'and if you *don't* mind, one from my mouth – *So*!'

Gip counselled me mutely for a moment, and then in a profound silence put away the four balls, resumed my reassuring finger, and nerved himself for the next event.

'We get all our smaller tricks in that way,' the shopman remarked.

I laughed in the manner of one who subscribes to a jest. 'Instead of going to the wholesale shop,' I said. 'Of course, it's cheaper.

'In a way,' the shopman said. 'Though we pay in the end. But not so heavily – as people suppose. . . . Our larger tricks, and our daily provisions and all the other things we want, we get out of that hat. . . . And you know, sir, if you'll excuse my saying it, there *isn't* a wholesale shop, not for Genuine Magic goods, sir. I don't know if you noticed our inscription – the Genuine Magic shop.' He drew a business-card from his cheek and handed it to me. 'Genuine,' he said, with his finger on the word, and added, 'There is absolutely no deception, sir.'

He seemed to be carrying out the joke pretty thoroughly, I thought.

He turned to Gip with a smile of remarkable affability. 'You, you know, are the Right Sort of Boy.'

I was surprised at his knowing that, because, in the interests of discipline, we keep it rather a secret even at home; but Gip received it in unflinching silence, keeping a steadfast eye on him.

'It's only the Right Sort of Boy gets through

that doorway.'

And as if by way of illustration, there came a rattling at the door, and a squeaking little voice could be faintly heard. 'Nyar! I *warn* a' go in there, Dad, I WARN a' go in there. Ny-a-a-ah!' and then the accents of a down-trodden parent, urging consolations and propitiations. 'It's locked, Edward,' he said.

'But it isn't,' said I.

'It is, sir,' said the shopman, 'always – for that sort of child,' and as he spoke we had a glimpse of the other youngster, a small, white face, pallid from sweet-eating and over-fatty food, and distorted by evil passions, a ruthless little egotist, pawing at the enchanted pane. 'It's no good, sir,' said the shopman, as I moved, with my natural helpfulness, doorward, and presently the spoilt child was carried off howling.

'How do you manage that?' I said, breathing more freely.

'Magic!' said the shopman, with a careless wave of the hand, and behold! sparks of coloured fire flew out of his fingers and vanished into the shadows of the shop.

'You were saying,' he said, addressing himself to Gip, 'before you came in, that you would like one of our "Buy One and Astonish your Friends' boxes?'

Gip, after a gallant effort, said 'Yes.'

'It's in your pocket.'

And leaning over the counter – he really had an

extraordinarily long body – this amazing person produced the article in the customary conjurer's manner. 'Paper,' he said, and took a sheet out of the empty hat with the springs; 'string', and behold his mouth was a string-box, from which he drew an unending thread, which when he had tied his parcel he bit off – and, it seemed to me, swallowed the ball of string. And then he lit a candle at the nose of one of the ventriloquist's dummies, stuck one of his fingers (which had become sealing-wax red) into the flame, and so sealed the parcel. 'Then there was the Disappearing Egg,' he remarked, and produced one from within my coat-breast and packed it, and also The Crying Baby, Very Human. I handed each parcel to Gip as it was ready, and he clasped them to his chest. He said very little, but his eyes were eloquent; the clutch of his arms was eloquent. He was the playground of unspeakable emotions. These, you know, were *real* Magics.

Then, with a start, I discovered something moving about in my hat – something soft and jumpy. I whipped it off, and a ruffled pigeon – no doubt a confederate – dropped out and ran on the counter, and went, I fancy, into a cardboard box behind the *papier-mâché* tiger.

'Tut, tut!' said the shopman, dexterously relieving me of my headdress; 'careless bird, and – as I live – nesting!'

He shook my hat, and shook out into his extended hand two or three eggs, a large marble, a watch, about half-a-dozen of the inevitable glass balls, and then crumpled, crinkled paper, more and more and more, talking all the time of the way in which people neglect to brush their hats *inside* as well as out, politely, of course, but with a certain personal application. 'All sorts of things accumulate, sir . . . Not *you*, of course, in particular . . . Nearly every customer . . . Astonishing what they carry about with them . . .' The crumpled paper rose and billowed on the counter more and more and more, until he was nearly hidden from us, until he was altogether hidden, and still his voice went on and on. 'We none of us know what the fair semblance of a human being may conceal, sir. Are we all then no better than brushed exteriors, whited sepulchres –'

His voice stopped – exactly like when you hit a neighbour's gramophone with a well-aimed brick, the same instant silence, and the rustle of the paper stopped, and everything was still . . .

'Have you done with my hat?' I said, after an interval.

There was no answer.

I stared at Gip, and Gip stared at me; and there were our distortions in the magic mirrors, looking very rum, and grave, and quiet . . .

'I think we'll go now,' I said. 'Will you tell me how much all this comes to? . . .

'I say,' I said, on a rather louder note, 'I want the bill; and my hat, please.'

It might have been a sniff from behind the paper pile. . .

'Let's look behind the counter, Gip,' I said. 'He's making fun of us.'

I led Gip round the head-wagging tiger, and what do you think there was behind the counter? No one at all! Only my hat on the floor, and a common conjurer's lop-eared white rabbit lost in meditation, and looking as stupid and crumpled as only a conjurer's rabbit can do. I resumed my hat, and the rabbit lolloped a lollop or so out of my way.

'Dad!' said Gip, in a guilty whisper.

'What is it, Gip?' said I.

'I *do* like this shop, Dad.'

'So should I,' I said to myself, 'if the counter wouldn't suddenly extend itself to shut one off from the door.' But I didn't call Gip's attention to that. 'Pussy!' he said, with a hand out to the rabbit as it came lolloping past us; 'Pussy, do Gip a magic!' and his eyes followed it as it squeezed through a door I had certainly not noticed a moment before. Then this door opened wider, and the man with one ear larger than the other appeared again. He was smiling still, but his eye met mine with something between amusement and defiance. 'You'd like to see our showroom, sir,' he said, with an innocent suavity. Gip tugged my finger forward. I glanced at the counter and met the shopman's eye again. I was beginning to think the magic just a little too genuine. 'We haven't *very* much time,' I said. But somehow we were inside the showroom before I could finish that.

'All goods of the same quality, said the shopman, rubbing his flexible hands together, 'and that is the Best. Nothing in the place that isn't genuine Magic, and warranted thoroughly rum. Excuse me, sir!'

I felt him pull at something that clung to my coat-sleeve, and then I saw he held a little, wriggling red demon by the tail – the little creature bit and fought and tried to get at his hand – and in a moment he tossed it carelessly behind a counter. No doubt the thing was only an image of twisted india-rubber, but for the moment! And his gesture was exactly that of a man who handles some petty biting bit of vermin. I glanced at Gip, but Gip was looking at a magic rocking-horse. I was glad he hadn't seen the thing. 'I say,' I said, in an undertone, and indicating Gip and the red demon with my eyes, 'you haven't many things like *that* about, have you?'

'None of ours! Probably brought it with you,' said the shopman – also in an undertone, and with a more dazzling smile than ever. 'Astonishing what people *will* carry about with them unawares!' And then to Gip, 'Do you see anything you fancy here?'

There were many things that Gip fancied there.

He turned to this astonishing tradesman with mingled

confidence and respect. 'Is that a Magic Sword?' he said.

'A Magic Toy Sword. It neither bends, breaks, nor cuts the fingers. It renders the bearer invincible in battle against anyone under eighteen. Half-a-crown to seven and sixpence, according to size. These panoplies on cards are for juvenile knights-errant and very useful – shield of safety, sandals of swiftness, helmet of invisibility.'

'Oh, Dad!' gasped Gip.

I tried to find out what they cost, but the shopman did not heed me. He had got Gip now; he had got him away from my finger; he had embarked upon the exposition of all his confounded stock, and nothing was going to stop him. Presently I saw with a qualm of distrust and something very like jealousy that Gip had hold of this person's finger as usually he has hold of mine. No doubt the fellow was interesting, I thought, and had an interestingly faked lot of stuff, really *good* faked stuff, still –

I wandered after them, saying very little, but keeping an eye on this prestidigital fellow. After all, Gip was enjoying it. And no doubt when the time came to go we should be able to go quite easily.

It was a long, rambling place, that showroom, a gallery broken up by stands and stalls and pillars, with archways leading off to other departments, in which the queerest-looking assistants loafed and stared at one, and with perplexing mirrors and curtains. So perplexing, indeed, were these that I was presently unable to make out the door by which we had come.

The shopman showed Gip magic trains that ran without steam or clockwork, just as you set the signals, and then some very, very valuable boxes of soldiers that all came alive directly you took off the lid and said – I myself haven't a very quick ear and it was a tongue-twisting sound, but Gip – he has his mother's ear – got it in no time. 'Bravo!' said the shopman, putting the men back into the box unceremoniously and handing it to Gip. 'Now,' said the shopman, and in a moment Gip had made them all alive again.

'You'll take that box?' asked the shopman.

'We'll take that box,' said I, 'unless you charge its full value. In which case it would need a Trust Magnate –'

'Dear heart! *No!*' and the shopman swept the little men back again, shut the lid, waved the box in the air, and there it was, in brown paper, tied up and – *with Gip's full name and address on the paper!*

The shopman laughed at my amazement.

'This is the genuine magic,' he said. 'The real thing.'

'It's almost too genuine for my taste,' I said again.

After that he fell to showing Gip tricks, odd tricks, and still odder the way they were done. He explained them, he turned them inside out, and there was the dear little chap nodding his busy bit of a head in the sagest manner.

I did not attend as well I might. 'Hey, presto!' said the Magic Shopman, and then would come the clear, small 'Hey, presto!' of the boy. But I was distracted by other things. It was being borne in upon me just how tremendously rum this place was; it was, so to speak, inundated by a sense of rumness. There was something vaguely rum about the fixtures even, about the ceiling, about the floor, about the casually distributed chairs. I had a queer feeling that whenever I wasn't looking at them straight they went askew, and moved about, and played a noiseless puss-in-the-corner behind my back. And the cornice had a serpentine design with mask – masks altogether too expressive for proper plaster.

Then abruptly my attention was caught by one of the odd-looking assistants. He was some way off and evidently unaware of my presence – I saw a sort of three-quarter length of him over a pile of toys and through an arch – and, you know, he was leaning against a pillar in an idle sort of way doing the most horrid things with his features. The particular horrid thing he did was with his nose. He did it just as though he was idle and wanted to amuse himself. First of all it was a short, blobby nose, and then suddenly he shot it out like a telescope, and then out it flew and became thinner and thinner until it was like a long, red, flexible whip. Like a thing in a nightmare it was! He flourished it about and flung it forth as a fly-fisher flings his line.

My instant thought was that Gip mustn't see him. I turned about, and there was Gip quite preoccupied with the shopman, and thinking no evil. They were whispering together and looking at me. Gip was standing on a stool, and the shopman was holding a sort of big drum in his hand.

'Hide and seek, Dad!' cried Gip. 'You're He!'

And before I could do anything to prevent it, the shopman had clapped the big drum over him.

I saw what was up directly. 'Take that off,' I cried, 'this instant! You'll frighten the boy. Take it off!'

The shopman with the unequal ears did so without a word, and held the big cylinder towards me to show its emptiness. And the stool was vacant! In that instant my boy had utterly disappeared! . . .

You know, perhaps, that sinister something that comes like a hand out of the unseen and grips your heart about. You know it takes your commonsense away and leaves you tense and deliberate, neither slow nor hasty, neither angry nor afraid. So it was with me.

I came up to this grinning shopman and kicked his stool aside.

'Stop this folly!' I said. 'Where is my boy?'

'You see,' he said, still displaying the drum's interior, 'there is no deception –'

I put out my hand to grip him, and he eluded me by a dexterous movement. I snatched again, and he turned from me and pushed open a door to escape. 'Stop!' I said, and he laughed, receding. I leapt after him – into utter darkness.

Thud!

'Lor' bless my 'eart! I didn't see you coming, sir!'

I was in Regent Street, and I had collided with a decent-looking working man; and a yard away, perhaps, and looking extremely perplexed with himself, was Gip. There was some sort of apology, and then Gip had turned and come to me with a bright little smile, as though for a moment he had missed me.

And he was carrying four parcels in his arm!

He secured immediate possession of my finger.

For the second I was rather at a loss. I stared round to see the door of the magic shop, and; behold, it was not there! There was no door, no shop, nothing, only the common pilaster between the shop where they sell pictures and the window with the chicks!

I did the only thing possible in that mental tumult; I walked straight to the kerbstone and held up my umbrella for a cab.

''Ansoms,' said Gip, in a note of culminating exultation.

I helped him in, recalled my address with an effort, and got in also. Something unusual proclaimed itself in my tailcoat pocket, and I felt and discovered a glass ball. With a petulant expression I flung it into the street.

Gip said nothing.

For a space neither of us spoke.

'Dad!' said Gip, at last, 'that *was* a proper shop!'

I came round with that to the problem of just how the whole thing had seemed to him. He looked completely undamaged – so far, good; he was neither scared nor unhinged, he was simply tremendously satisfied with the afternoon's entertainment, and there in his arms were the four parcels.

Confound it what could be in them?

'Um!' I said. 'Little boys can't go to shops like that every day.'

He received this with his usual stoicism, and for a moment I was sorry I was his father and not his mother, and so couldn't suddenly there, *coram publico*, in our hansom, kiss him. After all, I thought, the thing wasn't so very bad.

But it was only when we opened the parcels that I really began to be reassured. Three of them contained boxes of soldiers, quite ordinary lead soldiers, but of so good a quality as to make Gip altogether forget that originally these parcels had been Magic Tricks of the only genuine sort, and the fourth contained a kitten, a little living white kitten, in excellent health and appetite and temper.

I saw this unpacking with a sort of provisional relief. I hung about in the nursery for quite an unconscionable time . . .

That happened six months ago. And now I am beginning to believe it is all right. The kitten had only the magic natural to all kittens, and the soldiers seem as steady a company as any colonel could desire. And Gip?

The intelligent parent will understand that I have to go cautiously with Gip.

But I went so far as this one day. I said, 'How would you like your soldiers to come alive, Gip, and march about by themselves?'

'Mine do,' said Gip. 'I just have to say a word I know before I open the lid.'

'Then they march about alone?'

'Oh, *quite*, Dad. I shouldn't like them if they didn't do that.'

I displayed no unbecoming surprise, and since then I have taken occasion to drop in upon him once or twice, unannounced, when the soldiers were about, but so far I have never discovered them performing in anything like a magical manner . . .

It's so difficult to tell.

There's also a question of finance. I have an incurable habit of paying bills. I have been up and down Regent Street several times, looking for that shop. I am inclined to think, indeed, that in that matter honour is satisfied, and that, since Gip's name and address are known to them, I may very well leave it to these people, whoever they may be, to send in their bill in their own time.

* * *

THE VALLEY OF THE SPIDERS

TOWARDS midday the three pursuers came abruptly round a bend in the torrent bed upon the sight of a very broad and spacious valley. The difficult and winding trench of pebbles along which they had tracked the fugitives for so long expanded to a broad slope, and with a common impulse the three men left the trail, and rode to a low eminence set with olive-dun trees, and there halted, the two others, as became them, a little behind the man with the silver-studded bridle.

For a space they scanned the great expanse below them with eager eyes. It spread remoter and remoter, with only a few clusters of sere thorn bushes here and there, and the dim suggestions of some now waterless ravine to break its desolation of yellow grass. Its purple distances melted at last into the bluish slopes of the further hills – hills it might be of a greener kind – and above them invisibly supported, and seeming indeed to hang in the blue, were the snow-clad summits of mountains – that grew larger and bolder to the northwestward as the sides of the valley drew together. And westward the valley opened until a distant darkness under the sky told where the forests began. But the three men looked neither east nor west, but only steadfastly across the valley.

The gaunt man with the scarred lip was the first to speak. 'Nowhere,' he said, with a sigh of disappointment in his voice. 'But after all, they had a full day's start.'

'They don't know we are after them,' said the little man on the white horse.

'*She* would know,' said the leader bitterly, as if speaking to himself.

'Even then they can't go fast. They've got no beast but the mule, and all today the girl's foot has been bleeding –'

The man with the silver bridle flashed a quick intensity of rage on him. 'Do you think I haven't seen that?' he snarled.

'It helps, anyhow,' whispered the little man to himself.

The gaunt man with the scarred lip stared impassively. 'They can't be over the valley,' he said. 'If we ride hard –'

He glanced at the white horse and paused.

'Curse all white horses!' said the man with the silver bridle and turned to scan the beast his curse included.

The little man looked down between the melancholy ears of his steed.

'I did my best,' he said.

The two others stared again across the valley for a space. The gaunt man passed the back of his hand across the scarred lip.

'Come up!' said the man who owned the silver bridle, suddenly. The little man started and jerked his rein, and the horse hoofs of the three made a multitudinous faint pattering upon the withered grass as they turned back towards the trail . . .

They rode cautiously down the long slope before them, and so came through a waste of prickly twisted bushes and strange dry shapes of horny branches that grew amongst the rocks, into the level below. And there the trail grew faint, for the soil was scanty, and the only herbage was this scorched dead straw that lay upon the ground. Still, by hard scanning, by leaning beside the horse's neck and pausing ever and again, even these white men could contrive to follow after their prey.

There were trodden places, bent and broken blades of the coarse grass, and ever and again the sufficient intimation of a footmark. And once the leader saw a brown smear of blood where the half-caste girl may have trod. And at that under his breath he cursed her for a fool.

The gaunt man checked his leader's tracking, and the little man on the white horse rode behind, a man lost in a dream. They rode one after another, the man with the silver bridle led the way, and they spoke never a word. After a time it came to the little man on the white horse that the world was very still. He started out of his dream. Besides the minute noises of their horses and equipment, the whole great valley kept the brooding quiet of a painted scene.

Before him went his master and his fellow, each intently leaning forward to the left, each impassively moving with the paces of his horse; their shadows went before them – still, noiseless, tapering attendants; and nearer a crouched cool shape was his own. He looked about him. What was it had gone? Then he remembered the reverberation from the banks of the gorge and the perpetual accompaniment of shifting, jostling pebbles. And, moreover –? There was no breeze. That was it! What a vast, still place it was, a monotonous afternoon slumber. And the sky open and blank, except for a sombre veil of haze that had gathered in the upper valley.

He straightened his back, fretted with his bridle, puckered his lips to whistle, and simply sighed. He turned in his saddle for a time, and stared at the throat of the mountain gorge out of which they had come. Blank! Blank slopes on either side, with never a sign of a decent beast or tree – much less a man. What a land it was! What a wilderness! He dropped again into his former pose.

It filled him with a momentary pleasure to see a wry stick of purple black flash out into the form of a snake, and vanish amidst the brown. After all, the infernal valley *was* alive. And then, to rejoice him still more, came a breath across his face, a whisper that came and went, the faintest inclination of a stiff black-antlered bush upon a crest, the first intimations of a possible breeze. Idly he wetted his finger, and held it up.

He pulled up sharply to avoid a collision with the gaunt man, who had stopped at fault upon the trail. Just at that guilty moment he caught his master's eye looking towards him.

For a time he forced an interest in the tracking. Then, as they rode on again, he studied his master's shadow and hat and shoulder appearing and disappearing behind the gaunt man's nearer contours. They had ridden four days out of the very limits of the world into this desolate place, short of water, with nothing but a strip of dried meat under their saddles, over rocks and mountains, where surely none but these fugitives had ever been before – for *that!*

And all this was for a girl, a mere wilful child! And the man had whole cityfuls of people to do his basest bidding – girls, women! Why in the name of passionate folly *this* one in particular? asked the little man, and scowled at the world, and licked his parched lips with a blackened tongue. It was the way of the master, and that was all he knew. Just because she sought to evade him . . .

His eye caught a whole row of high plumed canes bending in unison, and then the tails of silk that hung before his neck flapped and fell. The breeze was growing stronger. Somehow it took the stiff stillness out of things – and that was well.

'Hullo!' said the gaunt man.

All three stopped abruptly.

'What?' asked the master. 'What?'

'Over there,' said the gaunt man, pointing up the valley.

'What?'

'Something coming towards us.'

And as he spoke a yellow animal crested a rise and came bearing down upon them. It was a big wild dog, coming before the wind, tongue out, at a steady pace, and running with such an intensity of purpose that he did not seem to see the horsemen he approached. He ran with his nose up, following, it was plain, neither scent nor quarry. As he drew nearer the little man felt for his sword. 'He's mad,' said the gaunt rider.

'Shout!' said the little man and shouted.

The dog came on. Then when the little man's blade was already out, it swerved aside and went panting by them and past. The eyes of the little man followed its flight. 'There was no foam,' he said. For a space the man with the silver-studded bridle stared up the valley. 'Oh, come on!' he cried at last. 'What does it matter?' and jerked his horse into movement again.

The little man left the insoluble mystery of a dog that fled from nothing but the wind, and lapsed into profound musings on human character. 'Come on!' he whispered to himself. 'Why should it be given to one man to say "Come on!" with that stupendous violence of effect. Always, all his life, the man with the silver bridle has been saying that. If *I* said it –!' thought the little man. But people marvelled when the master was disobeyed even in the wildest things. This half-caste girl seemed to him, seemed to everyone, mad – blasphemous almost. The little man, by way of comparison, reflected on the gaunt rider with the scarred lip, as stalwart as his master, as brave and, indeed, perhaps braver, and yet for him there was obedience, nothing but to give obedience duly and stoutly . . .

Certain sensations of the hands and knees called the little man back to more immediate things. He became aware of something. He rode up beside his gaunt fellow. 'Do you notice the horses?' he said in an undertone.

The gaunt face looked interrogation.

'They don't like this wind,' said the little man, and dropped behind as the man with the silver bridle turned upon him.

'It's all right,' said the gaunt-faced man.

They rode on again for a space in silence. The foremost two rode downcast upon the trail, the hindmost man watched the haze that crept down the vastness of the valley, nearer and nearer, and noted how the wind grew in strength moment by moment. Far away on the left he saw a line of dark bulks – wild hog perhaps, galloping down the valley, but of that he said nothing, nor did he remark again upon the uneasiness of the horses.

And then he saw first one and then a second great white ball, a great shining white ball like a gigantic head of thistledown, that drove before the wind athwart the path. These balls soared high in the air, and dropped and rose again and caught for a moment, and hurried on and passed, but at the sight of them the restlessness of the horses increased.

Then presently he saw that more of these drifting globes – and then soon very many more – were hurrying towards him down the valley.

They became aware of a squealing. Athwart the path a huge boar rushed, turning his head but for one instant to glance at them, and then hurtling on down the valley again. And at that, all three stopped and sat in their saddles, staring into the thickening haze that was coming upon them.

'If it were not for this thistledown –' began the leader.

But now a big globe came drifting past within a score of yards of them. It was really not an even sphere at all, but a vast, soft, ragged, filmy thing, a sheet gathered by the corners, an aerial jelly-fish, as it were, but rolling over and over as it advanced, and trailing long, cobwebby threads and streamers that floated in its wake.

'It isn't thistledown,' said the little man.

'I don't like the stuff,' said the gaunt man.

And they looked at one another.

'Curse it!' cried the leader. 'The air's full of it up there. If it keeps on at this pace long, it will stop us altogether.'

An instinctive feeling, such as lines out a herd of deer at the approach of some ambiguous thing, prompted them to turn their horses to the wind, ride forwards for a few paces, and stare at that advancing multitude of floating masses. They came on before the wind with a sort of smooth swiftness, rising and falling noiselessly, sinking to earth, rebounding high, soaring – all with a perfect unanimity, with a still, deliberate assurance.

Right and left of the horsemen the pioneers of this strange army passed. At one that rolled along the ground, breaking shapelessly and trailing out reluctantly into long grappling ribbons and bands, all three horses began to shy and dance. The master was seized with a sudden, unreasonable impatience. He cursed the drifting globes roundly. 'Get on!' he cried; 'get on! What do these things matter? How *can* they matter? Back to the trail!' He fell swearing at his horse and sawed the bit across its mouth.

He shouted aloud with rage. 'I will follow that trail, I tell you,' he cried. 'Where is the trail!'

He gripped the bridle of his prancing horse and searched amidst the grass. A long and clinging thread fell across his face, a grey streamer dropped about his bridle arm, some big, active thing with many legs ran down the back of his head. He looked up to discover one of those grey masses anchored as it were above him by these things and flapping out ends as a sail flaps when a boat comes about – but noiselessly.

He had an impression of many eyes, of a dense crew of squat bodies, of long, many-jointed limbs hauling at their mooring ropes to bring the thing down upon him. For a space he stared up, reining in his prancing horse with the instinct born of years of horsemanship. Then the flat of a sword smote his back, and a blade flashed overhead and cut the drifting balloon of spider-web free, and the whole mass lifted softly and drove clear and away.

'Spiders!' cried the voice of the gaunt man. 'The things are full of big spiders! Look, my lord!'

The man with the silver bridle still followed the mass that drove away.

'Look, my lord!'

The master found himself staring down at a red smashed thing on the ground that, in spite of partial obliteration, could still wriggle unavailing legs. Then when the gaunt man pointed to another mass that bore down upon them, he drew his sword hastily. Up the valley now it was like a fog bank torn to rags. He tried to grasp the situation.

'Ride for it!' the little man was shouting. 'Ride for it down the valley.'

What happened then was like the confusion of a battle. The man with the silver bridle saw the little man go past him slashing furiously at imaginary cobwebs, saw him cannon into the horse of the gaunt man and hurl it and its rider to earth. His own horse went a dozen paces before he could rein it in. Then he looked up to avoid imaginary dangers, and then back again to see a horse rolling on the ground, the gaunt man standing and slashing over it at a rent and fluttering mass of grey that streamed and wrapped about them both. And thick and fast as thistledown on waste land on a windy day in July, the cobweb masses were coming on.

The little man had dismounted, but he dared not release his horse. He was endeavouring to lug the struggling brute back with the strength of one arm, while with the other he slashed aimlessly. The tentacles of a second grey mass had entangled themselves with the struggle, and this second grey mass came to its moorings, and slowly sank.

The master set his teeth, gripped his bridle, lowered his head, and spurred his horse forward. The horse on the ground rolled over, there was blood and moving shapes upon the flanks, and the gaunt man suddenly leaving it, ran forward towards his master, perhaps ten paces. His legs were swathed and encumbered with grey; he made ineffectual movements with his sword. Grey streamers waved from him; there was a thin veil of grey across his face. With his left hand he beat at something on his body, and suddenly he stumbled and fell. He struggled to rise, and fell again, and suddenly, horribly, began to howl, 'Oh – ohoo, ohooh!'

The master could see the great spiders upon him, and others upon the ground.

As he strove to force his horse nearer to this gesticulating screaming grey object that struggled up and down, there came a clatter of hoofs, and the little man, in act of mounting, swordless, balanced on his belly athwart the white horse, and clutching its mane, whirled past. And again a clinging thread of grey gossamer swept across the master's face. All about him and over him, it seemed this drifting, noiseless cobweb circled and drew nearer him . . .

To the day of his death he never knew just how the event of that moment happened. Did he, indeed, turn his horse, or did it really of its own accord stampede after its fellow? Suffice it that in another second he was galloping full tilt down the valley with his sword whirling furiously overhead. And all about him on the quickening breeze, the spiders' airships, their air bundles and air sheets, seemed to him to hurry in a conscious pursuit.

Clatter, clatter, thud, thud – the man with the silver bridle rode, heedless of his direction, with his fearful face looking up now right, now left, and his sword arm ready to slash. And a few hundred yards ahead of him, with a tail of torn cobweb trailing behind him, rode the little man on the white horse, still but imperfectly in the saddle. The reeds bent before them, the wind blew fresh and strong, over his shoulder the master could see the webs hurrying to overtake . . .

He was so intent to escape the spiders' webs that only as his horse gathered together for a leap did he realize the ravine ahead. And then he realized it only to misunderstand and interfere. He was leaning forward on his horse's neck and sat up and back all too late.

But if in his excitement he had failed to leap, at any rate he had not forgotten how to fall. He was horseman again in mid-air. He came off clear with a mere bruise upon his shoulder, and his horse rolled, kicking spasmodic legs, and lay still. But the master's sword drove its point into the hard soil, and snapped clean across, as though Chance refused him any longer as her Knight, and the splintered end missed his face by an inch or so.

He was on his feet in a moment, breathlessly scanning the onrushing spider-webs. For a moment he was minded to run, and then thought of the ravine, and turned back. He ran aside once to dodge one drifting terror, and then he was swiftly clambering down the precipitous sides, and out of the touch of the gale.

There under the lee of the dry torrent's steeper banks he might crouch, and watch these strange, grey masses pass and pass in safety till the wind fell, and it became possible to escape. And there for a long time he crouched, watching the strange, grey, ragged masses trail their streamers across his narrowed sky.

Once a stray spider fell into the ravine close beside him – a full foot it measured from leg to leg, and its body was half a man's hand – and after he had watched its monstrous alacrity of search and escape for a little while, and tempted it to bite his broken sword, he lifted up his iron heeled boot and smashed it into a pulp. He swore as he did so, and for a time sought up and down for another.

Then presently, when he was sure these spider swarms could not drop into the ravine, he found a place where he could sit down, and sat and fell into deep thought and began after his manner to gnaw his knuckles and bite his nails. And from this he was moved by the coming of the man with the white horse.

He heard him long before he saw him, as a clattering of hoofs, stumbling footsteps, and a reassuring voice. Then the little man appeared, a rueful figure, still with a tail of white cobweb trailing behind him. They approached each other without speaking, without a salutation. The little man was fatigued and shamed to the pitch of hopeless bitterness, and came to a stop at last, face to face with his seated master. The latter winced a little under his dependant's eye. 'Well?' he said at last, with no pretence of authority.

'You left him!'

'My horse bolted.'

'I know. So did mine.'

He laughed at his master mirthlessly.

'I say my horse bolted,' said the man who once had a silver-studded bridle.

'Cowards both,' said the little man.

The other gnawed his knuckle through some meditative movements, with his eyes on his inferior.

'Don't call me a coward,' he said at length.

'You are a coward like myself.'

'A coward possibly. There is a limit beyond which every man must fear. That I have learnt at last. But not like yourself. That is where the difference comes in.'

'I never could have dreamt you would have left him. He saved your life two minutes before . . . Why are you our lord?'

The master gnawed his knuckles again, and his countenance was dark.

'No man calls me a coward,' he said. 'No . . . A broken sword is better than none . . . One spavined white horse cannot be expected to carry two men a four days' journey. I hate white horses, but this time it cannot be helped. You begin to understand me? . . . I perceive that you are minded, on the strength of what you have seen and fancy, to taint my reputation. It is men of your sort who unmake kings.

Besides which – I never liked you.'

'My lord!' said the little man.

'No,' said the master. '*No!*'

He stood up sharply as the little man moved. For a minute perhaps they faced one another. Overhead the spiders' balls went driving. There was a quick movement among the pebbles; a running of feet, a cry of despair, a gasp and a blow . . .

Towards nightfall the wind fell. The sun set in a calm serenity, and the man who had once possessed the silver bridle came at last very cautiously and by an easy slope out of the ravine again; but now he led the white horse that once belonged to the little man. He would have gone back to his horse to get his silver-mounted bridle again, but he feared night and a quickening breeze might still find him in the valley, and besides he disliked greatly to think he might discover his horse all swathed in cobwebs and perhaps unpleasantly eaten.

And as he thought of those cobwebs and of all the dangers he had been through, and the manner in which he had been preserved that day, his hand sought a little reliquary that hung about his neck, and he clasped it for a moment with heartfelt gratitude. As he did so his eyes went across the valley.

'I was hot with passion,' he said, 'and now she has met her

reward. They also, no doubt –'

And behold! Far away out of the wooded slopes across the valley, but in the clearness of the sunset distinct and unmistakable, he saw a little spire of smoke.

At that his expression of serene resignation changed to an amazed anger. Smoke? He turned the head of the white horse about, and hesitated. And as he did so a little rustle of air went through the grass about him. Far away upon some reeds swayed a tattered sheet of grey. He looked at the cobwebs; he looked at the smoke.

'Perhaps, after all, it is not them,' he said at last.

But he knew better.

After he had stared at the smoke for some time, he mounted the white horse.

As he rode, he picked his way amidst stranded masses of web. For some reason there were many dead spiders on the ground, and those that lived feasted guiltily on their fellow. At the sound of his horse's hoofs they fled.

Their time had passed. From the ground, without either a wind to carry them or a winding sheet ready, these things, for all their poison, could do him no evil.

He flicked with his belt at those he fancied came too near. Once, where a number ran together over a bare place, he was minded to dismount and trample them with his boots, but this impulse he overcame. Ever and again he turned in his saddle, and looked back at the smoke.

'Spiders,' he muttered over and over again. 'Spiders! Well, well . . . The next time I must spin a web.'

THE CRYSTAL EGG

THERE was, until a year ago, a little and very grimy-looking shop near Seven Dials, over which, in weatherworn yellow lettering, the name of 'C. Cave, Naturalist and Dealer in Antiquities', was inscribed. The contents of its window were curiously varied. They comprised some elephant tusks and an imperfect set of chessmen, beads and weapons, a box of eyes, two skulls of tigers and one human, several moth-eaten stuffed monkeys (one holding a lamp), an old-fashioned cabinet, a fly-blown ostrich egg or so, some fishing-tackle, and an extraordinarily dirty, empty glass fish-tank. There was also, at the moment the story begins, a mass of crystal, worked into the shape of an egg and brilliantly polished. And at that two people, who stood outside the window, were looking, one of them a tall, thin clergyman, the other a black-bearded young man of dusky complexion and unobtrusive costume. The dusky young man spoke with eager gesticulation, and seemed anxious for his companion to purchase the article.

While they were there, Mr Cave came into his shop, his beard still wagging with the bread and butter of his tea. When he saw these men and the object of their regard, his countenance fell. He glanced guiltily over his shoulder, and softly shut the door. He was a little old man, with pale face and peculiar watery blue eyes; his hair was a dirty grey, and he wore a shabby blue frock-coat, an ancient silk hat, and carpet slippers very much down at heel. He remained watching the two men as they talked. The clergyman went deep into his trouser pocket, examined a handful of money, and showed his teeth in an agreeable smile. Mr Cave seemed still more depressed when they came into the shop.

The clergyman, without any ceremony, asked the price of the crystal egg. Mr Cave danced glanced nervously towards the door leading into the parlour, and said five pounds. The clergyman protested that the price was high, to his companion as well as to Mr Cave – it was, indeed, very much more than Mr Cave had intended to ask, when he had stocked the article – and an attempt at bargaining ensued. Mr Cave stepped to the shop door, and held it open. 'Five pounds is my price,' he said, as though he wished to save himself the trouble of unprofitable discussion. As he did so, the upper portion of a woman's face appeared above the blind in the glass upper-panel of the door leading into the parlour, and stared curiously at the two customers. 'Five pounds is my price,' said Mr Cave, with a quiver in his voice.

The swarthy young man had so far remained a spectator, watching Cave keenly. Now he spoke. 'Give him five pounds,' he said. The clergyman glanced at him to see if he were in earnest, and, when he looked at Mr Cave again, he saw that the latter's face was white. 'It's a lot of money,' said the clergyman, and, diving into his pocket, began counting his resources. He had little more than thirty shillings, and he appealed to his companion, with whom he seemed to be on terms of considerable intimacy. This gave Mr Cave an opportunity of collecting his thoughts, and he began to explain in an agitated manner that the crystal was not, as a matter of fact, entirely free for sale. His two customers were naturally surprised at this, and inquired why he had not thought of that before he began to bargain. Mr Cave became confused, but he stuck to his story, that the crystal was not in the market that afternoon, that a probable purchaser of it had already appeared. The two, treating this as an attempt to raise the price still further, made as if they would leave the shop. But at this point the parlour door opened, and the owner of the dark fringe and the little eyes appeared.

She was a coarse-featured, corpulent woman, younger and very much larger than Mr Cave; she walked heavily, and her face was flushed. 'That crystal *is* for sale,' she said. 'And five pounds is a good enough price for it. I can't think what you're about, Cave, not to take the gentleman's offer!'

Mr Cave, greatly perturbed by the irruption, looked angrily at her over the rims of his spectacles, and, without excessive assurance, asserted his right to manage his business in his own way. An altercation began. The two customers watched the scene with interest and some amusement, occasionally assisting Mrs Cave with suggestions. Mr Cave, hard driven, persisted in a confused and impossible story of an inquiry for the crystal that morning, and his agitation became painful. But he stuck to his point with extraordinary persistence. It was the young Oriental who ended this curious controversy. He proposed that they should call again in the course of two days – so as to give the alleged inquirer a fair chance. 'And then we must insist,' said the clergyman. 'Five pounds.' Mrs Cave took it on herself to apologize for her husband, explaining that he was sometimes 'a little odd,' and as the two customers left, the couple prepared for a free discussion of the incident in all its bearings.

Mrs Cave talked to her husband with singular directness. The poor little man, quivering with emotion, muddled himself between his stories, maintaining on the one hand that he had another customer in view, and on the other asserting that the crystal was honestly worth ten guineas. 'Why did you ask five pounds?' said his wife. '*Do* let me manage my business my own way!' said Mr Cave.

Mr Cave had living with him a step-daughter and a stepson, and at supper that night the transaction was rediscussed. None of them had a high opinion of Mr Cave's business methods, and this action seemed a culminating folly.

'It's my opinion he's refused that crystal before,' said the step-son, a loose-limbed lout of eighteen.

'But *Five Pounds*!' said the step-daughter, an argumentative young woman of six-and-twenty.

Mr Cave's answers were wretched; he could only mumble weak assertions that he knew his own business best. They drove him from his half-eaten supper into the shop to close it for the night, his ears aflame and tears of vexation behind his spectacles. 'Why had he left the crystal in the window so long? The folly of it!' That was the trouble closest in his mind. For a time he could see no way of evading sale.

After supper his step-daughter and step-son smartened themselves up and went out and his wife retired upstairs to reflect upon the business aspects of the crystal, over a little sugar and lemon and so forth in hot water. Mr Cave went into the shop, and stayed there until late, ostensibly to make ornamental rockeries for goldfish cases but really for a private purpose that will be better explained later. The next day Mrs Cave found that the crystal had been removed from the window, and was lying behind some second-hand books on angling. She replaced it in a conspicuous position. But she did not argue further about it, as a nervous headache disinclined her from debate. Mr Cave was always disinclined. The day passed disagreeably. Mr Cave was, if anything, more absent-minded than usual, and uncommonly irritable withal. In the afternoon, when his wife was taking her customary sleep, he removed the crystal from the window again.

The next day Mr Cave had to deliver a consignment of dog-fish at one of the hospital schools, where they were needed for dissection. In his absence Mrs Cave's mind reverted to the topic of the crystal, and the methods of expenditure suitable to a windfall of five pounds. She had already devised some very agreeable expedients, among others a dress of green silk for herself and a trip to Richmond, when a jangling of the front door bell summoned her into the shop. The customer was an examination coach who came to complain of the non-delivery of certain frogs asked for the previous day. Mrs Cave did not approve of this particular branch of Mr Cave's business, and the gentleman, who had called in a somewhat aggressive mood, retired after a brief exchange of words – entirely civil so far as he was concerned. Mrs Cave's eye then naturally turned to the window; for the sight of the crystal was an assurance of the five pounds and of her dreams. What was her surprise to find it gone!

She went to the place behind the locker on the counter, where she had discovered it the day before. It was not there; and she immediately began an eager search about the shop.

When Mr Cave returned from his business with the dogfish, about a quarter to two in the afternoon, he found the shop in some confusion, and his wife, extremely exasperated and on her knees behind the counter, routing among his taxidermic material. Her face came up hot and angry over the counter, as the jangling bell announced his return, and she forthwith accused him of 'hiding it'.

'Hid *what?*' asked Mr Cave.

'The crystal!'

At that Mr Cave, apparently much surprised, rushed to the window. 'Isn't it here?' he said. 'Great Heavens! what has become of it?'

Just then, Mr Cave's step-son reentered the shop from the inner room – he had come home a minute or so before Mr Cave – and he was blaspheming freely. He was apprenticed to a second-hand furniture dealer down the road, but he had his meals at home, and he was naturally annoyed to find no dinner ready.

But, when he heard of the loss of the crystal, he forgot his meal, and his anger was diverted from his mother to his stepfather. Their first idea, of course, was that he had hidden it. But Mr Cave stoutly denied all knowledge of its fate – freely offering his bedabbled affidavit in the matter – and at last was worked up to the point of accusing, first, his wife and then his step-son of having taken it with a view to a private sale. So began an exceedingly acrimonious and emotional discussion, which ended for Mrs Cave in a peculiar nervous condition midway between hysterics and amuck, and caused the stepson to be half-an-hour late at the furniture establishment in the afternoon. Mr Cave took refuge from his wife's emotions in the shop.

In the evening the matter was resumed, with less passion and in a judicial spirit, under the presidency of the stepdaughter. The supper passed unhappily and culminated in a painful scene. Mr Cave gave way at last to extreme exasperation, and went out banging the front door violently. The rest of the family, having discussed him with the freedom his absence warranted, hunted the house from garret to cellar, hoping to light upon the crystal.

The next day the two customers called again. They were received by Mrs Cave almost in tears. It transpired that no one *could* imagine all that she had stood from Cave at various times in her married pilgrimage. . . . She also gave a garbled account of the disappearance. The clergyman and the Oriental laughed silently at one another, and said it was very extraordinary. As Mrs Cave seemed disposed to give them the complete history of her life they made to leave the shop. Thereupon Mrs Cave, still clinging to hope, asked for the clergyman's address, so that, if she could get anything out of Cave, she might communicate it. The address was duly given, but apparently was afterwards mislaid. Mrs Cave can remember nothing about it.

In the evening of that day, the Caves seem to have exhausted their emotions, and Mr Cave, who had been out in the afternoon, supped in a gloomy isolation that contrasted pleasantly with the impassioned controversy of the previous days. For some time matters were very badly strained in the Cave household, but neither crystal nor customer reappeared.

Now, without mincing the matter, we must admit that Mr Cave was a liar. He new knew perfectly well where the crystal was. It was in the rooms of Mr Jacoby Wace, Assistant Demonstrator at St Catherine's, Westbourne Hospital, Westbourne Street. It stood on the sideboard partially covered by a black velvet cloth, and beside a decanter of American whisky. It is from Mr Wace, indeed, that the particulars upon which this narrative is based were derived. Cave had taken off the thing to the hospital hidden in the dog-fish sack, and there had pressed the young investigator to keep it for him. Mr Wace was a little dubious at first. His relationship to Cave was peculiar. He had a taste for singular characters, and he had more than once invited the old man to smoke and drink in his rooms, and to unfold his rather amusing views of life in general and of his wife in particular. Mr Wace had encountered Mrs Cave, too, on occasions when Mr Cave was not at home to attend to him. He knew the constant interference to which Cave was subjected, and having weighed the story judicially, he decided to give the crystal a refuge. Mr Cave promised to explain the reasons for his remarkable affection for the crystal more fully on a later occasion, but he spoke distinctly of seeing visions therein. He called on Mr Wace the same evening.

He told a complicated story. The crystal he said had come into his possession with other oddments at the forced sale of another curiosity dealer's effects, and not knowing what its value might be, he had ticketed it at ten shillings. It had hung upon his hands at that price for some months, and he was thinking of 'reducing the figure', when he made a singular discovery.

At that time his health was very bad – and it must be borne in mind that, throughout all this experience, his physical condition was one of ebb – and he was in considerable distress by reason of the negligence, the positive ill-treatment even, he received from his wife and step-children. His wife was vain, extravagant, unfeeling, and had a growing taste for private drinking; his step-daughter was mean and over-reaching; and his step-son had conceived a violent dislike for him, and lost no chance of showing it. The requirements of his business pressed heavily upon him, and Mr Wace does not think that he was altogether free from occasional intemperance. He had begun life in a comfortable position, he was a man of fair education, and he suffered, for weeks at a stretch, from melancholia and insomnia. Afraid to disturb his family, he would slip quietly from his wife's side, when his thoughts became intolerable, and wander about the house. And about three o'clock one morning, late in August, chance directed him into the shop.

The dirty little place was impenetrably black except in one spot, where he perceived an unusual glow of light. Approaching this, he discovered it to be the crystal egg, which was standing on the corner of the counter towards the window. A thin ray smote through a crack in the shutters, impinged upon the object, and seemed as it were to fill its entire interior.

It occurred to Mr Cave that this was not in accordance with the laws of optics as he had known them in his younger days. He could understand the rays being refracted by the crystal and coming to a focus in its interior, but this diffusion jarred with his physical conceptions. He approached the crystal nearly, peering into it and round it, with a transient revival of the scientific curiosity that in his youth had determined his choice of a calling. He was surprised to find the light not steady, but writhing within the substance of the egg, as though that object was a hollow sphere of some luminous vapour. In moving about to get different points of view, he suddenly found that he had come between it and the ray, and that the crystal none the less remained luminous. Greatly astonished, he lifted it out of the light ray and carried it to the darkest part of the shop. It remained bright for some four or five minutes, when it slowly faded and went out. He placed it in the thin streak of daylight, and its luminousness was almost immediately restored.

So far, at least, Mr Wace was able to verify the remarkable story of Mr Cave. He has himself repeatedly held this crystal in a ray of light (which had to be of a less diameter than one millimetre). And in a perfect darkness, such as could be produced by velvet wrapping, the crystal did undoubtedly appear very faintly phosphorescent. It would seem, however, that the luminousness was of some exceptional sort, and not equally visible to all eyes; for Mr Harbinger – whose name will be familiar to the scientific reader in connection with the Pasteur Institute – was quite unable to see any light whatever. And Mr Wace's own capacity for its appreciation was out of comparison inferior to that of Mr Cave's. Even with Mr Cave the power varied very considerably: his vision was most vivid during states of extreme weakness and fatigue.

Now from the outset this light in the crystal exercised an irresistible fascination upon Mr Cave. And it says more for his loneliness of soul than a volume of pathetic writing could do, that he told no human being of his curious observations. He seems to have been living in such an atmosphere of petty spite that to admit the existence of a pleasure would have been to risk the loss of it. He found that as the dawn advanced, and the amount of diffused light increased, the crystal became to all appearance non-luminous. And for some time he was unable to see anything in it, except at night-time, in dark corners of the shop.

But the use of an old velvet cloth, which he used as a background for a collection of minerals, occurred to him, and by doubling this, and putting it over his head and hands, he was able to get a sight of the luminous movement within the crystal even in the day-time. He was very cautious lest he should be thus discovered by his wife, and he practised this occupation only in the afternoons, while she was asleep upstairs, and then circumspectly in a hollow under the counter. And one day, turning the crystal about in his hands, he saw something. It came and went like a flash, but it gave him the impression that the object had for a moment opened to him the view of a wide and spacious and strange country, and turning it about, he did, just as the light faded, see the same vision again.

Now, it would be tedious and unnecessary to state all the phases of Mr Cave's discovery from this point. Suffice that the effect was this: the crystal, being peered into at an angle of about 137 degrees from the direction of the illuminating ray, gave a clear and consistent picture of a wide and peculiar country-side. It was not dream-like at all; it produced a definite impression of reality, and the better the light the more real and solid it seemed. It was a moving picture: that is to say, certain objects moved in it, but slowly in an orderly manner like real things, and according as the direction of the lighting and vision changed, the picture changed also. It must, indeed, have been like looking through an oval glass at a view, and turning the glass about to get at different aspects.

Mr Cave's statements, Mr Wace assures me, were extremely circumstantial, and entirely free from any of that emotional quality that taints hallucinatory impressions. But it must be remembered that all the efforts of Mr Wace to see any similar clarity in the faint opalescence of the crystal were wholly unsuccessful, try as he would. The difference in intensity of the impressions received by the two men was very great, and it is quite conceivable that what was a view to Mr Cave was a mere blurred nebulosity to Mr Wace.

The view as Mr Cave described it, was invariably of an extensive plain, and he seemed always to be looking at it from a considerable height, as if from a tower or a mast. To the east and to the west the plain was bounded at a remote distance by vast reddish cliffs, which reminded him of those he had seen in some picture; but what the picture was Mr Wace was unable to ascertain. These cliffs passed north and south – he could tell the points of the compass by the stars that were visible of a night – receding in an almost illimitable perspective and fading into the mists of the distance before they met. He was nearer the eastern set of cliffs, on the occasion of his first vision the sun was rising over them, and black against the sunlight and pale against their shadow appeared a multitude of soaring forms that Mr Cave regarded as birds. A vast range of buildings spread below him; he seemed to be looking down upon them; and, as they approached the blurred and refracted edge of the picture, they became indistinct. There were also trees curious in shape, and in colouring, a deep mossy green and an exquisite grey, beside a wide and shining canal. And something great and brilliantly coloured flew across the picture. But the first time Mr Cave saw these pictures he saw only in flashes, his hands shook, his head moved, the vision came and went, and grew foggy and indistinct. And at first he had the greatest difficulty in finding the picture again once the direction of it was lost.

His next clear vision, which came about a week after the first, the interval having yielded nothing but tantalizing glimpses and some useful experience, showed him the view down the length of the valley. The view was different, but he had a curious persuasion, which his subsequent observations abundantly confirmed, that he was regarding this strange world from exactly the same spot, although he was looking in a different direction. The long façade of the great building, whose roof he had looked down upon before, was now receding in perspective. He recognized the roof. In the front of the façade was a terrace of massive proportions and extraordinary length, and down the middle of the terrace, at certain intervals, stood huge but very graceful masts, bearing small shiny objects which reflected the setting sun. The import of these small objects did not occur to Mr Cave until some time after, as he was describing the scene to Mr Wace. The terrace overhung a thicket of the most luxuriant and graceful vegetation, and beyond this was a wide grassy lawn on which certain broad creatures, in form like beetles but enormously larger, reposed. Beyond this again was a richly decorated causeway of pinkish stone; and beyond that, and lined with dense *red* weeds, and passing up the valley exactly parallel with the distant cliffs, was a broad and mirror-like expanse of water. The air seemed full of squadrons of great birds, manoeuvring in stately curves; and across the river was a multitude of splendid buildings, richly coloured and glittering with metallic tracery and facets, among a forest of moss-like and lichenous trees. And suddenly something flapped repeatedly across the vision, like the fluttering of a jewelled fan or the beating of a wing, and a face, or rather the upper part of a face with very large eyes, came as it were close to his own and as if on the other side of the crystal. Mr Cave was so startled and so impressed by the absolute reality of these eyes, that he drew his head back from the crystal to look behind it. He had become so absorbed in watching that he was quite surprised to find himself in the cool darkness of his little shop, with its familiar odour of methyl mustiness, and decay. And, as he blinked about him, the glowing crystal faded, and went out.

Such were the first general impressions of Mr Cave. The story is curiously direct and circumstantial. From the outset, when the valley first flashed momentarily on his senses, his imagination was strangely affected, and, as he began to appreciate the details of the scenes he saw, his wonder rose to the point of a passion. He went about his business listless and distraught, thinking only of the time when he should be able to return to his watching. And then a few weeks after his first sight of the valley came the two customers, the stress and excitement of their offer, and the narrow escape of the crystal from sale, as I have already told.

Now while the thing was Mr Cave's secret, it remained a mere wonder, a thing to creep to covertly and peep at, as a child might peep upon a forbidden garden. But Mr Wace has, for a young scientific investigator, a particularly lucid and consecutive habit of mind. Directly the crystal and its story came to him, and he had satisfied himself, by seeing the phosphorescence with his own eyes, that there really was a certain evidence for Mr Cave's statements, he proceeded to develop the matter systematically. Mr Cave was only too eager to come and feast his eyes on this wonderland he saw, and he came every night from half-past eight until half-past ten, and sometimes, in Mr Wace's absence, during the day. On Sunday afternoons, also, he came. From the outset, Mr Wace made copious notes, and it was due to his scientific method that the relation between the direction from which the initiating ray entered the crystal and the orientation of the picture was proved. And, by covering the crystal in a box perforated only with a small aperture to admit the exciting ray, and by substituting black holland for his buff blinds, he greatly improved the conditions of the observations; so that in a little while they were able to survey the valley in any direction they desired.

So having cleared the way, we may give a brief account of this visionary world within the crystal. The things were in all cases seen by Mr Cave, and the method of working was invariably for him to watch the crystal and report what he saw, while Mr Wace (who as a science student had learnt the trick of writing in the dark) wrote a brief note of his report. When the crystal faded, it was put into its box in the proper position and the electric light turned on. Mr Wace asked questions, and suggested observations to clear up difficult points. Nothing, indeed, could have been less visionary and more matter-of-fact.

The attention of Mr Cave had been speedily directed to the

bird-like creatures he had seen so abundantly present in each of his earlier visions. His first impression was soon corrected, and he considered for a time that they might represent a diurnal species of bat. Then he thought, grotesquely enough, that they might be cherubs. Their heads were round, and curiously human, and it was the eyes of one of them that had so startled him on his second observation. They had broad, silvery wings not feathered, but glistening almost as brilliantly as new-killed fish and with the same subtle play of colour, and these wings were not built on the plan of bird wing or bat, Mr Wace learned, but supported by curved ribs radiating from the body. (A sort of butterfly wing with curved ribs seems best to express their appearance.) The body was small, but fitted with two bunches of prehensile organs, like long tentacles, immediately under the mouth. Incredible as it appeared to Mr Wace, the persuasion at last became irresistible, that it was these creatures which owned the great quasi-human buildings and the magnificent garden that made the broad valley so splendid. And Mr Cave perceived that the buildings, with other peculiarities, no doors, but that the great circular windows, which opened freely, gave the creatures egress and entrance. They would alight upon their tentacles, fold their wings to a smallness almost rod-like, and hop into the interior. But among them was a multitude of smaller-winged creatures, like great dragonflies and moths and flying beetles, and across the greensward brilliantly coloured gigantic ground beetles crawled lazily to and fro. Moreover, on the causeways and terraces, large-headed creatures similar to the greater winged flies, but wingless, were visible, hopping busily upon their hand-like tangle of tentacles.

Allusion has already been made to the glittering objects upon masts that stood upon the terrace of the nearer building. It dawned upon Mr Cave, after regarding one of these masts very fixedly on one particular vivid day, that the glittering object there was a crystal exactly like that into which he peered. And a still more careful scrutiny convinced him that each one in a vista of nearly twenty carried a similar object.

Occasionally one of the larger flying creatures would flutter up to one, and, folding its wings and coiling a number of its tentacles about the mast, would regard the crystal fixedly for a space – sometimes as long as fifteen minutes. And a series of observations, made at the suggestions of Mr Wace, convinced both watchers that, so far as this visionary world was concerned, the crystal into which they peered actually stood at the summit of the end-most mast on the terrace, and that on one occasion at least one of these inhabitants of this other world had looked into Mr Cave's face while he was making these observations.

So much for the essential facts of this very singular story. Unless we dismiss it all as the ingenious fabrication of Mr Wace, we have to believe one of two things: either that Mr Cave's crystal was in two worlds at once, and that, while it was carried about in one, it remained stationary in the other, which seems altogether absurd; or else that it had some peculiar relation of sympathy with another and exactly similar crystal in this other world, so that what was seen in the interior of the one in this world was, under suitable conditions, visible to an observer in the corresponding crystal in the other world; and *vice versa*. At present, indeed, we do not know of any way in which two crystals could so come *en rapport*, but nowadays we know enough to understand that the thing is not altogether impossible. This view of the crystals as *en rapport* was the supposition that occurred to Mr Wace, and to me at least it seems extremely plausible. . .

And where was this other world? On this, also, the alert intelligence of Mr Wace speedily threw light. After sunset, the sky darkened rapidly – there was a very brief twilight interval indeed – and the stars shone out. They were recognizably the same as those we see, arranged in the same constellations. Mr Cave recognized the Bear, the Pleiades, Aldebaran, and Sirius: so that the other world must be somewhere in the solar system, and, at the utmost, only a few hundreds of millions of miles from our own. Following up this clue, Mr

Wace learned that the midnight sky was a darker blue even than our midwinter sky, and that the sun seemed a little smaller. *And there were two small moons!* 'like our moon but smaller, and quite differently marked,' one of which moved so rapidly that its motion was clearly visible as one regarded it. These moons were never high in the sky, but vanished as they rose: that is, every time they revolved they were eclipsed because they were so near their primary planet. And all this answers quite completely, although Mr Cave did not know it, to what must be the condition of things on Mars.

Indeed, it seems an exceedingly plausible conclusion that peering into this crystal Mr Cave did actually see the planet Mars and its inhabitants. And, if that be the case, then the evening star that shone so brilliantly in the sky of that distant vision was neither more nor less than our own familiar earth.

For a time the Martians – if they were Martians – do not seem to have known of Mr Cave's inspection. Once or twice one would come to peer, and go away very shortly to some other mast, as though the vision was unsatisfactory. During this time Mr Cave was able to watch the proceedings of these winged people without being disturbed by their attentions, and, although his report is necessarily vague and fragmentary, it is nevertheless very suggestive. Imagine the impression of humanity a Martian observer would get who, after a difficult process of preparation and with considerable fatigue to the eyes, was able to peer at London from the steeple of St Martin's Church for stretches, at longest, of four minutes at a time. Mr Cave was unable to ascertain if the winged Martians were the same as the Martians who hopped about the causeways and terraces, and if the latter could put on wings at will. He several times saw certain clumsy bipeds, dimly suggestive of apes, white and partially translucent, feeding among certain of the lichenous trees, and once some of these fled before one of the hopping, round-headed Martians. The latter caught one in its tentacles, and then the picture faded suddenly and left Mr Cave most tantalizingly in the dark. On another occasion a vast thing, that Mr Cave thought at first was some gigantic insect, appeared advancing along the causeway beside the canal with extraordinary rapidity. As this drew nearer Mr Cave perceived that it was a mechanism of shining metals and of extraordinary complexity. And then, when he looked again, it had passed out of sight.

After a time Mr Wace aspired to attract the attention of the Martians, and the next time that the strange eyes of one of them appeared close to the crystal Mr Cave cried out and sprang away, and they immediately turned on the light and began to gesticulate in a manner suggestive of signalling. But when at last Mr Cave examined the crystal again the

Martian had departed.

Thus far these observations had progressed in early November, and then Mr Cave, feeling that the suspicions of his family about the crystal were allayed, began to take it to and fro with him in order that, as occasion arose in the daytime or night, he might comfort himself with what was fast becoming the most real thing in his existence.

In December Mr Wace's work in connection with a forthcoming examination became heavy, the sittings were reluctantly suspended for a week, and for ten or eleven days – he is not quite sure which – he saw nothing of Cave. He then grew anxious to resume these investigations, and, the stress of his seasonal labours being abated, he went down to Seven Dials. At the corner he noticed a shutter before a bird fancier's window, and then another at a cobbler's. Mr Cave's shop was closed.

He rapped and the door was opened by the step-son in black. He at once called Mrs Cave, who was, Mr Wace could not but observe, in cheap but ample widow's weeds of the most imposing pattern. Without any very great surprise Mr Wace learnt that Cave was dead and already buried. She was in tears, and her voice was a little thick. She had just returned from Highgate. Her mind seemed occupied with her own prospects and the honourable details of the obsequies, but Mr Wace was at last able to learn the particulars of Cave's death. He had been found dead in his shop in the early morning, the day after his last visit to Mr Wace, and the crystal had been clasped in his stone-cold hands. His face was smiling, said Mrs Cave, and the velvet cloth from the minerals lay on the floor at his feet. He must have been dead five or six hours when he was found.

This came as a great shock to Wace, and he began to reproach himself bitterly for having neglected the plain symptoms of the old man's ill-health. But his chief thought was of the crystal. He approached that topic in a gingerly manner, because he knew Mrs Cave's peculiarities. He was dumbfounded to learn that it was sold.

Mrs Cave's first impulse, directly Cave's body had been taken upstairs, had been to write to the mad clergyman who had offered five pounds for the crystal, informing him of its recovery; but after a violent hunt in which her daughter joined her, they were convinced of the loss of his address. As they were without the means required to mourn and bury Cave in the elaborate style the dignity of an old Seven Dials inhabitant demands, they had appealed to a friendly fellow-tradesman in Great Portland Street. He had very kindly taken over a portion of the stock at a valuation. The valuation was his own and the crystal egg was included in one of the lots. Mr Wace, after a few suitable consolatory observations, a little off-handedly proffered perhaps, hurried at once to Great Portland Street. But there he learned that the crystal egg had already been sold to a tall, dark man in grey. And there the material facts in this curious, and to me at least very suggestive, story come abruptly to an end. The Great Portland Street dealer did not know who the tall dark man in grey was, nor had he observed him with sufficient attention to describe him minutely. He did not even know which way this person had gone after leaving the shop. For a time Mr Wace remained in the shop, trying the dealer's patience with hopeless questions, venting his own exasperation. And at last, realizing abruptly that the whole thing had passed out of his hands, had vanished like a vision of the night, he returned to his own rooms, a little astonished to find the notes he had made still tangible and visible upon his untidy table.

His annoyance and disappointment were naturally very great. He made a second call (equally ineffectual) upon the Great Portland Street dealer, and he resorted to advertisements in such periodicals as were likely to come into the hands of a bric-à-brac collector. He also wrote letters to *The Daily Chronicle* and *Nature*, but both those periodicals, suspecting a hoax, asked him to reconsider his action before they printed, and he was advised that such a strange story, unfortunately so bare of supporting evidence, might imperil his reputation as an investigator. Moreover, the calls of his proper work were urgent. So that after a month or so, save for an occasional reminder to certain dealers, he had reluctantly to abandon the quest of the crystal egg, and from that day to this it remains undiscovered. Occasionally, however, he tells me, and I can quite believe him, he has bursts of zeal in which he abandons his more urgent occupation and resumes the search.

Whether or not it will remain lost for ever, with the material and origin of it, are things equally speculative at the present time. If the present purchaser is a collector, one would have expected the inquiries of Mr Wace to have reached him through the dealers. He has been able to discover Mr Cave's clergyman and 'Oriental' – no other than the Rev. James Parker and the young Prince of Bosso-Kuni in Java. I am obliged to them for certain particulars. The object of the Prince was simply curiosity – and extravagance. He was so eager to buy, because Cave was so oddly reluctant to sell. It is just as possible that the buyer in the second instance was simply a casual purchaser and not a collector at all, and the crystal egg, for all I know, may at the present moment be within a mile of me, decorating a drawing-room or serving as a paper-weight – its remarkable functions all unknown. Indeed, it is partly with the idea of such a possibility that I have thrown this narrative into a form that will give it a chance of being read by the ordinary consumer of fiction.

My own ideas in the matter are practically identical with those of Mr Wace. I believe the crystal on the mast in Mars and the crystal egg of Mr Cave's to be in some physical, but at present quite inexplicable, way *en rapport*, and we both believe further that the terrestrial crystal must have been – possibly at some remote date – sent hither from that planet, in order to give the Martians a near view of our affairs. Possibly fellows to the crystals in the other masts are also on our globe. No theory of hallucination suffices for the facts.

THE CHRONIC ARGONAUTS

THE STORY FROM AN ESOTERIC POINT OF VIEW

Being the Account of Dr Nebogipfel's Sojourn in Llyddwdd

About half-a-mile outside the village of Llyddwdd by the road that goes up over the eastern flank of the mountain called Pen-y-pwll to Rwstog is a large farm-building known as the Manse. It derives this title from the fact that it was at one time the residence of the minister of the Calvinistic Methodists. It is a quaint, low, irregular erection, lying back some hundred yards from the railway, and now fast passing into a ruinous state.

Since its construction in the latter half of the last century this house has undergone many changes of fortune, having been abandoned long since by the farmer of the surrounding acres for less pretentious and more commodious headquarters. Among others Miss Carnot, 'the Gallic Sappho' at one time made it her home, and later on an old man named Williams became its occupier. The foul murder of this tenant by his two sons was the cause of its remaining for some considerable period uninhabited; with the inevitable consequence of its undergoing very extensive dilapidation.

The house had got a bad name, and adolescent man and Nature combined to bring swift desolation upon it. The fear of the Williamses which kept the Llyddwdd lads from gratifying their propensity to invade its deserted interior, manifested itself in unusually destructive resentment against its external breakables. The missiles with which they at once confessed and defied their spiritual dread, left scarcely a splinter of glass, and only battered relics of the old-fashioned leaden frames, in its narrow windows, while numberless shattered tiles about the house, and four or five black apertures yawning behind the naked rafters in the roof, also witnessed vividly to the energy of their trajection. Rain and wind thus had free way to enter the empty rooms and work their will there, old Time aiding and abetting. Alternately soaked and desiccated, the planks of flooring and wainscot warped apart strangely, split here and there, and tore themselves away in paroxysms of rheumatic pain from the rust-devoured nails that had once held them firm. The plaster of walls and ceiling, growing green-black with a rain-fed crust of lowly life, parted slowly from the fermenting laths; and large fragments thereof falling down inexplicably in tranquil hours, with loud concussion and clatter, gave strength to the popular superstition that old Williams and his sons were fated to re-enact their fearful tragedy until the final judgment. White roses and daedal creepers, that Miss Carnot had first adorned the walls with, spread now luxuriantly over the lichen-filmed tiles of the roof, and in slender graceful sprays timidly invaded the ghostly cobweb-draped apartments. Fungi, sickly pale, began to displace and uplift the bricks in the cellar floor; while on the rotting wood everywhere they clustered, in all the glory of the purple and mottled crimson, yellow-brown and hepatite. Woodlice and ants, beetles and moths, winged and creeping things innumerable, found each day a more congenial home among the ruins; and after them in ever-increasing multitudes swarmed the blotchy toads. Swallows and martins built every year more thickly in the silent, airy, upper chambers. Bats and owls struggled for the crepuscular corners of the lower rooms. Thus, in the Spring of the year eighteen hundred and eighty-seven, was Nature taking over, gradually but certainly, the tenancy of the old Manse. 'The house was falling into decay,' as men who do not appreciate the application of human derelicts to other beings' use would say, 'surely and swiftly.' But it was destined nevertheless to shelter another human tenant before its final dissolution.

There was no intelligence of the advent of a new inhabitant in quiet Llyddwdd. He came without a solitary premonition out of the vast unknown into the sphere of minute village observation and gossip. He fell into the Llyddwdd world, as it were, like a thunderbolt falling in the daytime. Suddenly, out of nothingness, he *was*. Rumour, indeed, vaguely averred that he was seen to arrive by a certain train from London, and to walk straight without hesitation to the old Manse, giving neither explanatory word nor sign to mortal as to his purpose there: but then the same fertile source of information also hinted that he was first beheld skimming down the slopes of steep Pen-y-pwll with exceeding swiftness, riding, as it appeared to the intelligent observer, upon an instrument not unlike a sieve and that he entered the house by the chimney. Of these conflicting reports, the former was the first to be generally circulated, but the latter, in view of the bizarre presence and eccentric ways of the newest inhabitant, obtained wider credence. By whatever means he arrived, there can be no doubt that he was in, and in possession of the Manse, on the first of May; because on the morning of that day he was inspected by Mrs Morgan ap Lloyd Jones, and subsequently by the numerous persons her report brought up the mountain slope, engaged in the curious occupation of nailing sheet-tin across the void window sockets of his new domicile—'blinding his house', as Mrs Morgan ap Lloyd Jones not inaptly termed it.

He was a small-bodied, sallow faced little man, clad in a close-fitting garment of some stiff, dark material, which Mr Parry Davies the Llyddwdd shoemaker, opined was leather. His aquiline nose, thin lips, high cheek-ridges, and pointed chin, were all small and mutually well proportioned; but the bones and muscles of his face were rendered excessively prominent and distinct by his extreme leanness. The same cause contributed to the sunken appearance of the large eager-looking grey eyes, that gazed forth from under his phenomenally wide and high forehead. It was this latter feature that most powerfully attracted the attention of an observer. It seemed to be great beyond all preconceived ratio to the rest of his countenance. Dimensions, corrugations, wrinkles, venation, were alike abnormally exaggerated. Below it his eyes glowed like lights in some cave at a cliff's foot. It so over-powered and suppressed the rest of his face as to give an *unhuman* appearance almost, to what would otherwise have been an unquestionably handsome profile. The lank black hair that hung unkempt before his eyes served to increase rather than conceal this effect, by adding to unnatural altitude a suggestion of hydrocephalic projection: and the idea of something ultra human was furthermore accentuated by the temporal arteries that pulsated visibly through his transparent yellow skin. No wonder, in view even of these things, that among the highly and over-poetical Cymric of Llyddwdd the sieve theory of arrival found considerable favour.

It was his bearing and actions, however, much more than his personality, that won over believers to the warlock notion of matters. In almost every circumstance of life the observant villagers soon found his ways were not only not *their* ways, but altogether inexplicable upon any theory of motives they could conceive. Thus, in a small matter at the beginning, when Arthur Price Williams, eminent and famous in every tavern in Caernarvonshire for his social gifts, endeavoured, in choicest Welsh and even choicer English, to inveigle the stranger into conversation over the sheet-tin performance, he failed utterly. Inquisitional supposition, straightforward enquiry, offer of assistance, suggestion of method, sarcasm, irony, abuse, and at last, gage of battle, though shouted with much effort from the road hedge, went unanswered and apparently unheard. Missile weapons, Arthur Price Williams found, were equally unavailing for the purpose of introduction, and the gathered crowd dispersed with unappeased curiosity and suspicion. Later in the day, the swarth apparition was seen striding down the mountain road towards the village, hatless, and with such swift width of step and set resolution of countenance, that Arthur Price Williams, beholding him from afar from the Pig and Whistle doorway was seized with dire consternation, and hid behind the Dutch oven in the kitchen till he was past. Wild panic also smote the school-house as the children were coming out, and drove them indoors like leaves before a gale. He was merely seeking the provision shop, however, and erupted thencefrom after a prolonged stay, loaded with a various armful of blue parcels, a loaf, herrings, pigs' trotters, salt pork, and a black bottle, with which he returned in the same swift projectile gait to the Manse. His way of shopping was to name, and to name simply, without solitary other word of explanation, civility or request, the article he required.

The shopkeeper's crude meteorological superstitions and inquisitive commonplaces, he seemed not to hear, and he might have been esteemed deaf if he had not evinced the promptest attention to the faintest relevant remark. Consequently it was speedily rumoured that he was determined to avoid all but the most necessary human intercourse. He lived altogether mysteriously, in the decaying manse, without mortal service or companionship, presumably sleeping on planks or litter, and either preparing his own food or eating it raw. This, coupled with the popular conception of the haunting patricides, did much to strengthen the popular supposition of some vast gulf between the newcomer and common humanity. The only thing that was inharmonious with this idea of severance from mankind was a constant flux of crates filled with grotesquely contorted glassware, cases of brazen and steel instruments, huge coils of wire, vast iron and fire-clay implements, of inconceivable purpose, jars and phials labelled in black and scarlet—POISON, huge packages of books, and gargantuan rolls of cartridge paper, which set in towards his Llyddwdd quarters from the outer world. The apparently hieroglyphic inscriptions on these various consignments revealed at the profound scrutiny of Pugh Jones that the style and title of the new inhabitant was Dr Moses Nebogipfel, Ph.D., F.R.S., N.W.R., PAID: at which discovery much edification was felt, especially among the purely Welsh-speaking community. Further than this, these arrivals, by their evident unfitness for any allowable mortal use, and inferential diabolicalness, filled the neighbourhood with a vague horror and lively curiosity, which were greatly augmented by the extraordinary phenomena, and still more extraordinary accounts thereof, that followed their reception in the Manse.

The first of these was on Wednesday, the fifteenth of May, when the Calvinistic Methodists of Llyddwdd had their annual commemoration festival; on which occasion, in accordance with custom, dwellers in the surrounding parishes of Rwstog, Pen-y-garn, Caergyllwdd, Llanrdd, and even distant Llanrwst flocked into the village. Popular thanks to Providence were materialised in the usual way, by means of plum-bread and butter, mixed tea, *terza*, consecrated flirtations, kiss-in-the-ring, rough-and-tumble football, and vituperative political speechmaking. About half-past eight the fun began to tarnish, and the assembly to break up; and by nine numerous couples and occasional groups were wending their way in the darkling along the hilly Llyddwdd and Rwstog road. It was a calm warm night; one of those nights when lamps, gas and heavy sleep seem stupid ingratitude to the Creator. The zenith sky was an ineffable deep lucent blue, and the evening star hung golden in the liquid darkness of the west. In the north-north-west, a faint phosphorescence marked the sunken day. The moon was just rising, pallid and gibbous over the huge haze-dimmed shoulder of Pen-y-pwll. Against the wan eastern sky, from the vague outline of the mountain slope, the Manse stood out black, clear and solitary. The stillness of the twilight had hushed the myriad murmurs of the day. Only the sounds of footsteps and voices and laughter, that came fitfully rising and falling from the roadway, and an intermittent hammering in the darkened dwelling, broke the silence. Suddenly a strange whizzing, buzzing whirr filled the night air, and a bright flicker glanced across the dim path of the wayfarers. All eyes were turned in astonishment to the old Manse. The house no longer loomed a black featureless block but was filled to overflowing with light. From the gaping holes in the roof, from chinks and fissures amid tiles and brickwork, from every gap which Nature or man had pierced in the crumbling old shell, a blinding blue-white glare was streaming, beside which the rising moon seemed a disc of opaque sulphur. The thin mist of the dewy night had caught the violet glow and hung, unearthly smoke, over the colourless blaze. A strange turmoil and outcrying in the old Manse now began, and grew ever more audible to the clustering spectators, and therewith came clanging loud impacts against the window-guarding tin. Then from the gleaming roof-gaps of the house suddenly vomited forth a wonderous swarm of heteromerous living things—swallows, sparrows, martins, owls, bats, insects in visible multitudes, to hang for many minutes a noisy, gyring, spreading cloud over the black gables and chimneys . . . and then slowly to thin out and vanish away in the night.

As this tumult died away the throbbing humming that had first arrested attention grew once more in the listener's hearing, until at last it was the only sound in the long stillness. Presently, however, the road gradually awoke again to the beating and shuffling of feet, as the knots of Rwstog people, one by one, turned their blinking eyes from the dazzling whiteness and, pondering deeply, continued their homeward way.

The cultivated reader will have already discerned that this phenomenon, which sowed a whole crop of uncanny thoughts in the minds of these worthy folk, was simply the installation of the electric light in the Manse. Truly, this last vicissitude of the old house was its strangest one. Its revival to mortal life was like the raising of Lazarus. From that hour forth, by night and day, behind the tin-blinded windows, the tamed lightning illuminated every corner of its quickly changing interior. The almost frenzied energy of the lank-haired, leather-clad little doctor swept away into obscure holes and corners and common destruction, creeper sprays, toadstools, rose leaves, birds' nests, birds' eggs, cobwebs, and all the coatings and lovingly fanciful trimmings with which that maternal old dotard, Dame Nature, had tricked out the decaying house for its lying in state. The magneto-electric apparatus whirred incessantly amid the vestiges of the wainscoted diningroom, where once the eighteenth-century tenant had piously read morning prayer and eaten his Sunday dinner; and in the place of his sacred symbolical sideboard was a nasty heap of coke. The oven of the bakehouse supplied substratum and material for a forge, whose snorting, panting bellows, and intermittent, ruddy spark-laden blast made the benighted, but Bible-lit Welsh women murmur in liquid Cymric, as they hurried by: 'Whose breath kindleth coals, and out of his mouth is a flame of fire.' For the idea these good people formed of it was that a tame, but occasionally restive, leviathan had been added to the terrors of the haunted house. The constantly increasing accumulation of pieces of machinery, big brass castings, block tin, casks, crates, and packages of innumerable articles, by their demands for space, necessitated the sacrifice of most of the slighter partitions of the house, and the beams and flooring of the upper chambers were also mercilessly sawn away by the tireless scientist in such a way as to convert them into mere shelves and corner brackets of the atrial space between cellars and rafters. Some of the sounder planking was utilised in the making of a rude broad table, upon which files and heaps of geometrical diagrams speedily accumulated. The production of these latter seemed to be the object upon which the mind of Dr Nebogipfel was so inflexibly set. All other circumstances of his life were made entirely subsidiary to this one occupation. Strangely complicated traceries of lines they were—plans, elevations, sections by surfaces and solids, that, with the help of logarithmic mechanical apparatus and involved curvigraphical machines, spread swiftly under his expert hands over yard after yard of paper. Some of these symbolised shapes he despatched to London, and they presently returned, *realised*, in forms of brass and ivory, and nickel and mahogany. Some of them he himself translated into solid models of metal and wood; occasionally casting the metallic ones in moulds of sand, but often laboriously hewing them out of the block for greater precision of dimension. In this second process, among other appliances, he employed a steel circular saw set with diamond powder and made to rotate with extraordinary swiftness, by means of steam and multiplying gear. It was this latter thing, more than all else, that filled Llyddwdd with a sickly loathing of the Doctor as a man of blood and darkness. Often in the silence of midnight—for the newest inhabitant heeded the sun but little in his incessant research—the awakened dwellers around Pen-y-pwll would hear, what was at first a complaining murmur, like the groaning of a wounded man, '*gurr*-urr-urr-URR', rising by slow gradations in pitch and intensity to the likeness of a voice in despairing passionate protest, and at last ending abruptly in a sharp piercing shriek that rang in the ears for hours afterwards and begot numberless gruesome dreams.

The mystery of all these unearthly noises and inexplicable phenomena, the Doctor's inhumanly brusque bearing and evident uneasiness when away from his absorbing occupation, his entire and jealous seclusion, and his terrifying behaviour to certain officious intruders, roused popular resentment and curiously to the highest, and a plot was already on foot to make some sort of popular inquisition (probably accompanied by an experimental ducking) into his proceedings, when the sudden death of the hunchback Hughes in a fit, brought matters to an unexpected crisis. It happened in broad daylight, in the roadway just opposite the Manse. Half a dozen people witnessed it. The unfortunate creature was seen to fall suddenly and roll about on the pathway, struggling violently, as it appeared to the spectators, with some invisible assailant. When assistance reached him he was purple in the face and his blue lips were covered with a glairy foam. He died almost as soon as they laid hands on him.

Owen Thomas, the general practitioner, vainly assured the excited crowd which speedily gathered outside the Pig and Whistle, whither the body had been carried, that death was unquestionably natural. A horrible zymotic suspicion had gone forth that the deceased was the victim of Dr Nebogipfel's imputed aerial powers. The contagion was with the news that passed like a flash through the village and set all Llyddwdd seething with a fierce desire for action against the worker of this iniquity. Downright superstition, which had previously walked somewhat modestly about the village, in the fear of ridicule and the Doctor, now appeared boldly before the sight of all men, clad in the terrible majesty of truth. People who had hitherto kept entire silence as to their fears of the imp-like philosopher suddenly discovered a fearsome pleasure in whispering dread possibilities to kindred souls, and from whispers of possibilities their sympathy-fostered utterances soon developed into unhesitating asserverations in loud and even high-pitched tones. The fancy of a captive leviathan, already alluded to, which had up to now been the horrid but secret joy of a certain conclave of ignorant old women, was published to all the world as indisputable fact; it being stated, on her own authority, that the animal had, on one occasion, chased Mrs Morgan ap Lloyd Jones almost into Rwstog. The story that Nebogipfel had been heard within the Manse chanting, in conjunction with the Williamses, horrible blasphemy, and that a 'black flapping thing, of the size of a young calf', had thereupon entered the gap in the roof, was universally believed in. A grisly anecdote, that owed its origination to a stumble in the churchyard, was circulated, to the effect that the Doctor had been caught ghoulishly tearing with his long white fingers at a new-made grave. The numerously attested declaration that Nebogipfel and the murdered Williams had been seen hanging the sons on a ghostly gibbet, at the back of the house, was due to the electric illumination of a fitfully wind-shaken tree. A hundred like stories hurtled thickly about the village and darkened the moral atmosphere. The Reverend Elijah Ulysses Cook, hearing of the tumult, sallied forth to allay it, and narrowly escaped drawing on himself the gathering lightning.

By eight o'clock (it was Monday the twenty-second of July) a grand demonstration had organised itself against the 'necromancer'. A number of bolder hearts among the men formed the nucleus of the gathering, and at nightfall Arthur Price Williams, John Peters, and others brought torches and raised their spark-raining flames aloft with curt ominous suggestions. The less adventurous village manhood came straggling late to the rendezvous, and with them the married women came in groups of four or five, greatly increasing the excitement of the assembly with their shrill hysterical talk and active imaginations. After these the children and young girls, overcome by undefinable dread, crept quietly out of the too silent and shadowy houses into the yellow glare of the pine knots, and the tumultuary noise of the thickening people. By nine, nearly half the Llyddwdd population was massed before the Pig and Whistle. There was a confused murmur of many tongues, but above all the stir and chatter of the growing crowd could be heard the coarse, cracked voice of the blood-thirsty old fanatic, Pritchard, drawing a congenial lesson from the fate of the four hundred and fifty idolators of Carmel.

Just as the church clock was beating out the hour, an occultly originated movement up hill began, and soon the whole assembly, men, women, and children, was moving in a fear-compacted mass, towards the ill-fated doctor's abode. As they left the brightly-lit public house behind them, a quavering female voice began singing one of those grim-sounding canticles that so satisfy the Calvinistic ear. In a wonderfully short time, the tune had been caught up, first by two or three, and then by the whole procession, and the manifold shuffling of heavy shoon grew swiftly into rhythm with the beats of the hymn. When, however, their goal rose, like a blazing star, over the undulation of the road, the volume of the chanting suddenly died away, leaving only the voices of the ringleaders, shouting indeed now somewhat out of tune, but, if anything, more vigorously than before. Their persistence and example nevertheless failed to prevent a perceptible breaking and slackening of the pace, as the Manse was neared, and when the gate was reached, the whole crowd came to a dead halt. Vague fear for the future had begotten the courage that had brought the villagers thus far: fear for the present now smothered its kindred birth. The intense blaze from the gaps in the death-like silent pile lit up rows of livid, hesitating faces: and a smothered, frightened sobbing broke out among the children. 'Well,' said Arthur Price Williams, addressing Jack Peters, with an expert assumption of the modest discipleship, 'what do we do *now*, Jack?' But Peters was regarding the Manse with manifest dubiety, and ignored the question. The Llyddwdd witch-find seemed to be suddenly aborting.

At this juncture old Pritchard suddenly pushed his way forward, gesticulating weirdly with his bony hands and long arms. '*What!*' he shouted, in broken notes, 'fear ye to smite when the Lord hateth? *Burn* the warlock!' And seizing a flambeau from Peters, he flung open the rickety gate and strode on down the drive, his torch leaving a coiling trail of scintillant sparks on the night wind. 'Burn the warlock,' screamed a shrill voice from the wavering crowd, and in a moment the gregarious human instinct had prevailed. With an outburst of incoherent, threatening voice, the mob poured after the fanatic.

Woe betide the Philosopher now! They expected barricaded doors; but with a groan of a conscious insufficiency, the hinge-rusted portals swung at the push of Pritchard. Blinded by the light, he hesitated for a second on the threshold, while his followers came crowding up behind him.

Those who were there say that they saw Dr Nebogipfel, standing in the toneless electric glare, on a peculiar erection of brass and ebony and ivory; and that he seemed to be smiling at them, half pityingly and half scornfully, as it is said martyrs are wont to smile. Some assert, moreover, that by his side was sitting a tall man, clad in ravenswing, and some even aver that this second man—whom others deny—bore on his face the likeness of the Reverend Elijah Ulysses Cook, while others declare that he resembled the description of the murdered Williams. Be that as it may, it must now go unproven for ever, for suddenly a wonderous thing smote the crowd as it swarmed in through the entrance. Pritchard pitched headlong on the floor senseless. While shouts and shrieks of anger, changed in mid utterance to yells of agonising fear, or to the mute gasp of heart-stopping horror: and then a frantic rush was made for the doorway.

For the calm, smiling doctor, and his quiet, black-clad companion, and the polished platform which upbore them, had vanished before their eyes!

HOW AN ESOTERIC STORY BECAME POSSIBLE

A silvery-foliaged willow by the side of a mere. Out of the cress-spangled waters below, rise clumps of sedge-blades, and among them glows the purple fleur-de-lys, and sapphire vapour of forget-me-nots. Beyond is a sluggish stream of water reflecting the intense blue of the moist Fenland sky; and beyond that a low osier-fringed eyot. This limits all the visible universe, save some scattered pollards and spear-like poplars showing against the violet distance. At the foot of the willow reclines the Author watching a copper butterfly fluttering from iris to iris.

Who can fix the colours of the sunset? Who can take a cast of flame? Let him essay to register the mutations of mortal thought as it wanders from a copper butterfly to the disembodied soul, and thence passes to spiritual motions and the vanishing of Dr Moses Nebogipfel and the Rev. Elijah Ulysses Cook from the world of sense.

As the author lay basking there and speculating, as another once did under the Budh tree, on mystic transmutations, a presence became apparent. There was a somewhat on the eyot between him and the purple horizon—an opaque reflecting entity, making itself dimly perceptible by reflection in the water to his averted eyes. He raised them in curious surprise.

What was it?

He stared in stupefied astonishment at the apparition, doubted, blinked, rubbed his eyes, stared again, and believed. It was solid, it cast a shadow, and it upbore two men. There was white metal in it that blazed in the noontide sun like incandescent magnesium, ebony bars that drank in the light, and white parts that gleamed like polished ivory. Yet withal it seemed unreal. The thing was not square as a machine ought to be, but all awry: it was twisted and seemed falling over, hanging in two directions, as those queer crystals called triclinic hang; it seemed like a machine that had been crushed or warped; it was suggestive and not confirmatory, like the machine of a disordered dream. The men, too, were dreamlike. One was short, intensely sallow, with a strangely-shaped head, and clad in a garment of dark olive green, the other was, grotesquely out of place, evidently a clergyman of the Established Church, a fair-haired, pale-faced respectable-looking man.

Once more doubt came rushing in on the author. He sprawled back and stared at the sky, rubbed his eyes, stared at the willow wands that hung between him and the blue, closely examined his hands to see if his eyes had any new things to relate about them, and then sat up again and stared at the eyot. A gentle breeze stirred the osiers; a white bird was flapping its way through the lower sky. The machine of the vision had vanished! It was an illusion—a projection of the subjective—an assertion of the immateriality of mind. 'Yes,' interpolated the sceptic faculty, 'but *how comes it that the clergyman is still there?*'

The clergyman had not vanished. In intense perplexity the author examined this black-coated phenomenon as he stood regarding the world with hand-shaded eyes. The author knew the periphery of that eyot by heart, and the question that troubled him was, 'Whence?' The clergyman looked as Frenchmen look when they land at Newhaven—intensely travel-worn; his clothes showed rubbed and seamy in the bright day. When he came to the edge of the island and shouted a question to the author, his voice was broken and trembled. 'Yes,' answered the author, 'it is an island. *How did you get there?*'

But the clergyman, instead of replying to this asked a very strange question.

He said 'Are you in the nineteenth century?' The author made him repeat that question before he replied. 'Thank heaven,' cried the clergyman rapturously. Then he asked very eagerly for the exact date.

'August the ninth, eighteen hundred and eighty-seven,' he repeated after the author. 'Heaven be praised!' and sinking down on the eyot so that the sedges hid him, he audibly burst into tears.

Now the author was mightily surprised at all this, and going a certain distance along the mere, he obtained a punt, and getting into it he hastily poled to the eyot where he had last seen the clergyman. He found him lying insensible among the reeds, and carried him in his punt to the house where he lived, and the clergyman lay there insensible for ten days.

Meanwhile, it became known that he was the Rev. Elijah Cook, who had disappeared from Llyddwdd with Dr Moses Nebogipfel three weeks before.

On August 19th, the nurse called the author out of his study to speak to the invalid. He found him perfectly sensible, but his eyes were strangely bright, and his face was deadly pale. 'Have you found out who I am?' he asked.

'You are the Rev. Elijah Ulysses Cook, Master of Arts, of Pembroke College, Oxford, and Rector of Llyddwdd, near Rwstog, in Caernarvon.'

He bowed his head. 'Have you been told anything of how I came here?'

'I found you among the reeds,' I said. He was silent and thoughtful for a while. 'I have a deposition to make. Will you take it? It concerns the murder of an old man named Williams, which occurred in 1862, this disappearance of Dr Moses Nebogipfel, the abduction of a ward in the year 4003—'

The author stared.

'The year of our Lord 4003,' he corrected. 'She would come. Also several assaults on public officials in the years 17,901 and 2.'

The author coughed.

'The years 17,901 and 2, and valuable medical, social, and physiographical data for all time.'

After a consultation with the doctor, it was decided to have the deposition taken down, and this is which constitutes the remainder of the story of the Chronic Argonauts.

On August 29th, 1887, the Rev Elijah Cook died. His body was conveyed to Llyddwdd, and buried in the churchyard there.

THE ESOTERIC STORY BASED ON THE CLERGYMAN'S DEPOSITIONS

The Anachronic Man

Incidentally it has been remarked in the first part, how the Reverend Elijah Ulysses Cook attempted and failed to quiet the superstitious excitement of the villagers on the afternoon of the memorable twenty-second of July. His next proceeding was to try and warn the unsocial philosopher of the dangers which impended. With this intent he made his way from the rumour-pelted village, through the silent, slumbrous heat of the July afternoon, up the slopes of Pen-y-pwll, to the old Manse. His loud knocking at the heavy door called forth dull resonance from the interior, and produced a shower of lumps of plaster and fragments of decaying touchwood from the rickety porch, but beyond this the dreamy stillness of the summer mid-day remained unbroken. Everything was so quiet as he stood there expectant, that the occasional speech of the haymakers a mile away in the fields, over towards Rwstog, could be distinctly heard. The reverend gentleman waited, then knocked again, and waited again, and listened, until the echoes and the patter of rubbish had melted away into the deep silence, and the creeping in the blood-vessels of his ears had become oppressively audible, swelling and sinking with sounds like the confused murmuring of a distant crowd, and causing a suggestion of anxious discomfort to spread slowly over his mind.

Again he knocked, this time loud, quick blows with his stick, and almost immediately afterwards, leaning his hand against the door, he kicked the panels vigorously. There was a shouting of echoes, a protesting jarring of hinges, and then the oaken door yawned and displayed, in the blue blaze of the electric light, vestiges of partitions, piles of planking and straw, masses of metal, heaps of papers and overthrown apparatus, to the rector's astonished eyes. 'Doctor Nebogipfel, excuse my intruding,' he called out, but the only response was a reverberation among the black beams and shadows that hung dimly above. For almost a minute he stood there, leaning forward over the threshold, staring at the glittering mechanisms, diagrams, books, scattered indiscriminately with broken food, packing cases, heaps of coke, hay, and microcosmic lumber, about the undivided house cavity; and then, removing his hat and treading stealthily, as if the silence were a sacred thing, he stepped into the apparently deserted shelter of the Doctor.

His eyes sought everywhere, as he cautiously made his way through the confusion, with a strange anticipation of finding Nebogipfel hidden somewhere in the sharp black shadows among the litter, so strong in him was an indescribable sense of perceiving presence. This feeling was so vivid that, when, after an abortive exploration, he seated himself upon Nebogipfel's diagram-covered bench, it made him explain in a forced hoarse voice to the stillness—'He is not here. I have something to say to him. I must wait for him.' It was so vivid, too, that the trickling of some grit down the wall in the vacant corner behind him made him start round in a sudden perspiration. There was nothing visible there, but turning his head back, he was stricken rigid with horror by the swift, noiseless apparition of Nebogipfel, ghastly pale, and with red stained hands, crouching upon a strange-looking metallic platform, and with his deep grey eyes looking intently into the visitor's face.

Cook's first impulse was to yell out his fear, but his throat was paralysed, and he could only stare fascinated at the bizarre countenance that had thus clashed suddenly into visibility. The lips were quivering and the breath came in short convulsive sobs. The un-human forehead was wet with perspiration, while the veins were swollen, knotted and purple. The Doctor's red hands, too, he noticed, were trembling, as the hands of slight people tremble after intense muscular exertion, and his lips closed and opened as if he, too, had a difficulty in speaking as he gasped, 'Who—what do you do here?'

Cook answered not a word, but stared with hair erect, open mouth, and dilated eyes, at the dark red unmistakeable smear that streaked the pure ivory and gleaming nickel and shining ebony of the platform.

'What are you doing here?' repeated the doctor, raising himself. 'What do you want?'

Cook gave a convulsive effort. 'In Heaven's name, *what* are you?' he gasped; and then black curtains came closing in from every side, sweeping the squatting, dwarfish phantasm that reeled before him into rayless, voiceless night.

The Reverend Elijah Ulysses Cook recovered his perceptions to find himself lying on the floor of the old Manse, and Doctor Nebogipfel, no longer blood-stained and with all trace of his agitation gone, kneeling by his side and bending over him with a glass of brandy in his hand. 'Do not be alarmed, sir,' said the philosopher with a faint smile, as the clergyman opened his eyes. 'I have not treated you to a disembodied spirit, or anything nearly so extraordinary . . . may I offer you this?'

The clergyman submitted quietly to the brandy, and then stared perplexed into Nebogipfel's face, vainly searching his memory for what occurrences had preceded his insensibility. Raising himself at last, into a sitting posture, he saw the oblique mass of metals that had appeared with the doctor, and immediately all that happened flashed back upon his mind. He looked from this structure to the recluse, and from the recluse to the structure.

'There is absolutely no deception, sir,' said Nebogipfel with the slightest trace of mockery in his voice. 'I lay no claim to work in matters spiritual. It is a *bona fide* mechanical contrivance, a thing emphatically of this sordid world. Excuse me—just one minute.' He rose from his knees, stepped upon the mahogany platform, took a curiously curved lever in his hand and pulled it over. Cook rubbed his eyes. *There* certainly was no deception. The doctor and the machine had vanished.

The reverend gentleman felt no horror this time, only a slight nervous shock, to see the doctor presently re-appear 'in the twinkling of an eye' and get down from the machine. From that he walked in a straight line with his hands behind his back and his face downcast, until his progress was stopped by the intervention of a circular saw; then, turning round sharply on his heel, he said:

'I was thinking while I was . . . away . . . Would you like to come? I should greatly value a companion.'

The clergyman was still sitting, hatless, on the floor. 'I am afraid,' he said slowly, 'you will think me stupid—'

'Not at all,' interrupted the doctor. 'The stupidity is mine. You desire to have all this explained . . . wish to know where I am going first. I have spoken so little with men of this age for the last ten years or more that I have ceased to make due allowances and concessions for other minds. I will do my best, but that I fear will be very unsatisfactory. It is a long story . . . do you find that floor comfortable to sit on? If not, there is a nice packing case over there, or some straw behind you, or this bench—the diagrams are done with now, but I am afraid of the drawing pins. You may sit on the Chronic Argo!'

'No, thank you,' slowly replied the clergyman, eyeing that

deformed structure thus indicated, suspiciously; 'I am *quite* comfortable here.'

'Then I will begin. Do you read fables? Modern ones?'

'I am afraid I must confess to a good deal of fiction,' said the clergyman deprecatingly. 'In Wales the ordained ministers of the sacraments of the Church have perhaps *too* large a share of leisure—'

'Have you read the Ugly Duckling?'

'Hans Christian Andersen's—yes—in my childhood.'

'A wonderful story—a story that has ever been full of tears and heart swelling hopes for me, since first it came to me in my lonely boyhood and saved me from unspeakable things. That story, if you understand it well, will tell you almost all that you should know of me to comprehend how that machine came to be thought of in a mortal brain . . . Even when I read that simple narrative for the first time, a thousand bitter experiences had begun the teaching of my isolation among the people of my birth—I knew the story was for me. The ugly duckling that proved to be a swan, that lived through all contempt and bitterness, to float at last sublime. From that hour forth, I dreamt of meeting with my kind, dreamt of encountering that sympathy I knew was my profoundest need. Twenty years I lived in that hope, lived and worked, lived and wandered, loved even, and at last, despaired. Only once among all those millions of wondering, astonished, indifferent, contemptuous, and insidious faces that I met with in that passionate wandering, looked *one* upon me as I desired . . . looked—'

He paused. The Reverend Cook glanced up into his face, expecting some indication of the deep feeling that had sounded in his last words. It was downcast, clouded, and thoughtful, but the mouth was rigidly firm.

'In short, Mr Cook, I discovered that I was one of those superior Cagots called a genius—a man born out of my time—a man thinking the thoughts of a wiser age, doing things and believing things that men now *cannot* understand, and that in the years ordained to me there was nothing but silence and suffering for my soul—unbroken solitude, man's bitterest pain. I knew I was an Anachronic Man; my age was still to come. One filmy hope alone held me to life, a hope to which I clung until it had become a certain thing. Thirty years of unremitting toil and deepest thought among the hidden things of matter and form and life, and then *that*, the Chronic Argo, *the ship that sails through time*, and now I go to join my generation, to journey through the ages till my time has come.'

THE CHRONIC ARGO

Dr Nebogipfel paused, looked in sudden doubt at the clergyman's perplexed face. 'You think that sounds mad,' he said, 'to travel through time?'

'It certainly jars with accepted opinions,' said the clergyman, allowing the faintest suggestion of controversy to appear in his intonation, and speaking apparently to the Chronic Argo. Even a clergyman of the Church of England you see can have a suspicion of illusions at times.

'It certainly *does* jar with accepted opinions,' agreed the philosopher cordially. 'It does more than that—it defies accepted opinions to mortal combat. Opinions of all sorts, Mr Cook—Scientific Theories, Laws, Articles of Belief, or, to come to elements, Logical Premises, Ideas, or whatever you like to call them—all are, from the infinite nature of things, so many diagrammatic caricatures of the ineffable—caricatures altogether to be avoided save where they are necessary in the shaping of results—as chalk outlines are necessary to the painter and plans and sections to the engineer. Men, from the exigencies of their being, find this hard to believe.'

The Rev. Elijah Ulysses Cook nodded his head with the quiet smile of one whose opponent has unwittingly given a point.

'It is as easy to come to regard ideas as complete reproductions of entities as it is to roll off a log. Hence it is that almost all civilised men believe in the *reality* of the Greek geometrical conceptions.'

'Oh! pardon me, sir,' interrupted Cook. 'Most men know that a geometrical point has no existence in matter, and the same with a geometrical line. I think you underrate . . .'

'Yes, yes, *those* things are recognised,' said Nebogipfel calmly; 'but now . . . a cube. Does that exist in the material universe?'

'Certainly.'

'An instantaneous cube?'

'I don't know what you intend by that expression.'

'Without any other sort of extension; a body having length, breadth, and thickness, exists?'

'What other sort of extension *can* there be?' asked Cook, with raised eyebrows.

'Has it never occurred to you that no form can exist in the material universe that has no extension in time? . . . Has it never glimmered upon your consciousness that nothing stood between men and a geometry of four dimensions—length, breadth, thickness, and *duration*—but the inertia of opinion, the impulse from the Levantine philosophers of the bronze age?'

'Putting it that way,' said the clergyman, 'it does look as though there was a flaw somewhere in the notion of tridimensional being; but' . . . He became silent, leaving that sufficiently eloquent 'but' to convey all the prejudice and distrust that filled his mind.

'When we take up this new light of a fourth dimension and reexamine our physical science in its illumination,' continued Nebogipfel, after a pause, 'we find ourselves no longer limited by hopeless restriction to a certain beat of time—to our own generation. Locomotion along lines of duration—chronic navigation comes within the range, first, of geometrical theory, and then of practical mechanics. There *was* a time when men could only move horizontally and in their appointed country. The clouds floated above them, unattainable things, mysterious chariots of those fearful gods who dwelt among the mountain summits. Speaking practically, men in those days were restricted to motion in two dimensions; and even there circumambient ocean and hypoborean fear bound him in. But those times were to pass away. First, the keel of Jason cut its way between the Symplegades, and then in the fulness of time, Columbus dropped anchor in a bay of Atlantis. Then man burst his bidimensional limits, and invaded the third dimension, soaring with Montgolfier into the clouds, and sinking with a diving bell into the purple treasure-caves of the waters. And now another step, and the hidden past and unknown future are before us. We stand upon a mountain summit with the plains of the ages spread below.'

Nebogipfel paused and looked down at his hearer.

The Reverend Elijah Cook was sitting with an expression of strong distrust on his face. Preaching much had brought home certain truths to him very vividly, and he always suspected rhetoric. 'Are those things figures of speech,' he asked; 'or am I to take them as precise statements? Do you speak of travelling through time in the same way as one might speak of Omnipotence making His pathway on the storm, or do you—a—mean what you say?'

Dr Nebogipfel smiled quietly. 'Come and look at these diagrams,' he said, and then with elaborate simplicity he commenced to explain again to the clergyman the new quadridimensional geometry. Insensibly Cook's aversion passed away, and seeming impossibility grew possible, now that such tangible things as diagrams and models could be brought forward in evidence. Presently he found himself asking questions, and his interest grew deeper and deeper as Nebogipfel slowly and with precise clearness unfolded the beautiful order of his strange invention. The moments slipped away unchecked, as the Doctor passed on to the narrative of his research, and it was with a start of surprise that the clergyman noticed the deep blue of the dying twilight through the open doorway.

'The voyage,' said Nebogipfel concluding his history, 'will be full of undreamt-of dangers—already in one brief essay I have stood in the very jaws of death—but it is also full of the divinest promise of undreamt-of joy. Will you come? Will you walk among the people of the Golden Years? . . .'

But the mention of death by the philosopher had brought flooding back to the mind of Cook, all the horrible sensations of that first apparition.

'Dr Nebogipfel . . . one question?' He hesitated. 'On your hands . . . *Was it blood?*'

Nebogipfel's countenance fell. He spoke slowly.

'When I had stopped my machine, I found myself in this room as it used to be. *Hark!*'

'It is the wind in the trees towards Rwstog.'

'It sounded like the voices of a multitude of people singing . . . when I had stopped I found myself in this room as it used to be. An old man, a young man, and a lad were sitting at a table—reading some book together. I stood behind them unsuspected. "Evil spirits assailed him," read the old man; "but it is written, 'to him that overcometh shall be given life eternal'. They came as entreating friends, but he endured through all their snares. They came as principalities and powers, but he defied them in the name of the King of Kings. Once even it is told that in his study, while he was translating the New Testament into German, the Evil One himself appeared before him . . ." Just then the lad glanced timorously round, and with a fearful wail fainted away . . .

'The others sprang at me . . . It was a fearful grapple . . . The old man clung to my throat, screaming "Man or Devil, I defy thee . . ."

'I could not help it. We rolled together on the floor . . . the knife his trembling son had dropped came to my hand . . . Hark!'

He paused and listened, but Cook remained staring at him in the same horror-stricken attitude he had assumed when the memory of the blood-stained hands had rushed back over his mind.

'Do you hear what they are crying? *Hark!*'

Burn the warlock! Burn the murderer!

'Do you hear? There is no time to be lost.'

Slay the murderer of cripples. Kill the devil's claw!

'Come! Come!'

Cook, with a convulsive effort, made a gesture of repugnance and strode to the doorway. A crowd of black figures roaring towards him in the red torchlight made him recoil. He shut the door and faced Nebogipfel.

The thin lips of the Doctor curled with a contemptuous sneer. 'They will kill you if you stay,' he said; and seizing his unresisting vistior by the wrist, he forced him towards the glittering machine. Cook sat down and covered his face with his hands.

In another moment the door was flung open, and old Pritchard stood blinking on the threshold.

A pause. A hoarse shout changing suddenly into a sharp shrill shriek.

A thunderous roar like the bursting forth of a great fountain of water.

The voyage of the Chronic Argonauts had begun.

The Inexperienced Ghost

The scene amidst which Clayton told his last story comes back very vividly to my mind. There he sat, for the greater part of the time, in the corner of the authentic settle by the spacious open fire, and Sanderson sat beside him smoking the Broseley clay that bore his name. There was Evans, and that marvel among actors, Wish, who is also a modest man. We had all come down to the Mermaid Club that Saturday morning, except Clayton, who had slept there overnight – which indeed gave him the opening of his story. We had golfed until golfing was invisible; we had dined, and we were in that mood of tranquil kindliness when men will suffer a story. When Clayton began to tell one, we naturally supposed he was lying. It may be that indeed he was lying – of that the reader will speedily be able to judge as well as I. He began, it is true, with an air of matter-of-fact anecdote, but that we thought was only the incurable artifice of the man.

"I say!" he remarked, after a long consideration of the upward rain of sparks from the log that Sanderson had thumped, "you know I was alone here last night?"

"Except for the domestics," said Wish.

"Who sleep in the other wing," said Clayton. "Yes. Well—" He pulled at his cigar for some little time as though he still hesitated about his confidence. Then he said, quite quietly, "I caught a ghost!"

"Caught a ghost, did you?" said Sanderson. "Where is it?"

And Evans, who admires Clayton immensely and has been four weeks in America, shouted, "*Caught* a ghost, did you, Clayton? I'm glad of it! Tell us all about it right now."

Clayton said he would in a minute, and asked him to shut the door.

He looked apologetically at me. "There's no eavesdropping, of course, but we don't want to upset our very excellent service with any rumours of ghosts in the place. There's too much shadow and oak panelling to trifle with that. And this, you know, wasn't a regular ghost. I don't think it will come again – ever."

"You mean to say you didn't keep it?" said Sanderson.

"I hadn't the heart to," said Clayton.

And Sanderson said he was surprised.

We laughed, and Clayton looked aggrieved. "I know," he said, with the flicker of a smile, "but the fact is it really *was* a ghost, and I'm as sure of it as I am that I am talking to you now. I'm not joking. I mean what I say."

Sanderson drew deeply at his pipe, with one reddish eye on Clayton, and then emitted a thin jet of smoke more eloquent than many words.

Clayton ignored the comment. "It is the strangest thing that has ever happened in my life. You know I never believed in ghosts or anything of the sort, before, ever; and then, you know, I bag one in a corner; and the whole business is in my hands."

He meditated still more profoundly and produced and began to pierce a second cigar with a curious little stabber he affected.

"You talked to it?" asked Wish.

"For the space, probably, of an hour."

"Chatty?" I said, joining the party of the sceptics.

"The poor devil was in trouble," said Clayton, bowed over his cigar-end and with the very faintest note of reproof.

"Sobbing?" someone asked.

Clayton heaved a realistic sight at the memory. "Good Lord!" he said, "yes." And then, "Poor fellow! Yes."

"Where did you strike it?" asked Evans, in his best

American accent.

"I never realised," said Clayton, ignoring him, "the poor sort of thing a ghost might be," and he hung us up again for a time, while he sought for matches in his pocket and lit and warmed to his cigar.

"I took an advantage," he reflected at last.

We were none of us in a hurry. "A character," he said, "remains just the same character for all that it's been disembodied. That's a thing we too often forget. People with a certain strength or fixity of purpose may have ghosts of a certain strength and fixity of purpose – most haunting ghosts, you know, must be as one-idea'd as monomaniacs and as obstinate as mules to come back again and again. This poor creature wasn't." He suddenly looked up rather queerly, and his eye went round the room. "I say it," he said, "in all kindliness, but that is the plain truth of the case. Even at the first glance he struck me as weak."

He punctuated with the help of his cigar.

"I came upon him, you know, in the long passage. His back was towards me and I saw him first. Right off I knew him for a ghost. He was transparent and whitish; clean through his chest I could see the glimmer of the little window at the end. And not only his physique but his attitude struck me as being weak. He looked, you know, as though he didn't know in the slightest whatever he meant to do. One hand was on the panelling and the other fluttered to his mouth. Like – *so!*"

"What sort of physique?" said Sanderson.

"Lean. You know that sort of young man's neck that has two great flutings down the back, here and here – so! And a little, meanish head with scrubby hair and rather bad ears. Shoulders bad, narrower than the hips; turndown collar, ready-made short jacket, trousers baggy and a little frayed at the heels. That's how he took me. I came very quietly up the staircase. I did not carry a light, you know – the candles are on the landing table and there is that lamp – and I was in my list slippers, and I saw him as I came up. I stopped dead at that – taking him in. I wasn't a bit afraid. I think that in most of these affairs one is never nearly so afraid or excited as one imagines one would be. I was surprised and interested. I thought, 'Good Lord! Here's a ghost at last! And I haven't believed for a moment in ghosts during the last five-and-twenty years.'"

"Um," said Wish.

"I suppose I wasn't on the landing a moment before he found out I was there. He turned on me sharply, and I saw the face of an immature young man, a weak nose, a scrubby little moustache, a feeble chin. So for an instant we stood – he looking over his shoulder at me – and regarded one another. Then he seemed to remember his high calling. He turned round, drew himself up, projected his face, raised his arms, spread his hands in approved ghost fashion – came towards me. As he did so his little jaw dropped, and he emitted a faint, drawn-out 'Boo.' No, it wasn't – not a bit dreadful. I'd dined. I'd had a bottle of champagne, and being all alone, perhaps two or three – perhaps even four or five – whiskies, so I was as solid as rocks and no more frightened than if I'd been assailed by a frog. 'Boo!' I said. 'Nonsense. You don't belong to *this* place. What are you doing here?'

"I could see him wince. 'Boo – oo,' he said.

" 'Boo – be hanged! Are you a member?' I said: and just to show I didn't care a pin for him I stepped through a corner of him and made to light my candle. 'Are you a member?' I repeated, looking at him sideways.

"He moved a little so as to stand clear of me, and his bearing became crestfallen. 'No,' he said, in answer to the persistent interrogation of my eye; 'I'm not a member – I'm a ghost.'

" 'Well, that doesn't give you the run of the Mermaid Club. Is there anyone you want to see, or anything of that sort?' And doing it as steadily as possible for fear that he should mistake the carelessness of whisky for the distraction of fear, I got my candle alight. I turned on him, holding it. 'What are you doing here?' I said.

"He had dropped his hands and stopped his booing, and

there he stood, abashed and awkward, the ghost of a weak, silly, aimless young man. 'I'm haunting,' he said.

" 'You haven't any business to,' I said in a quiet voice.

" 'I'm a ghost,' he said, as if in defence.

" 'That may be, but you haven't any business to haunt here. This is a respectable private club; people often stop here with nursemaids and children, and, going about in the careless way you do, some poor little mite could easily come upon you and be scared out of her wits. I suppose you didn't think of that?'

" 'No, sir,' he said, 'I didn't.'

" 'You should have done. You haven't any claim on the place, have you? Weren't murdered here, or anything of that sort?"

" 'None, sir; but I thought as it was old and oak-panelled—'

" 'That's *no* excuse.' I regarded him firmly. 'Your coming here is a mistake,' I said, in a tone of friendly superiority. I feigned to see if I had my matches, and then looked up at him frankly. 'If I were you I wouldn't wait for cock-crow – I'd vanish right away.'

"He looked embarrassed. 'The fact *is*, sir—' he began.

" 'I'd vanish,' I said, driving it home.

" 'The fact is, sir, that – somehow – I can't.'

" 'You *can't?*'

" 'No, sir. There's something I've forgotten. I've been hanging about here since midnight last night, hiding in the cupboards of the empty bedrooms and things like that. I'm flurried. I've never come haunting before, and it seems to put me out.'

" 'Put you out?'

" 'Yes, sir. I've tried to do it several times, and it doesn't come off. There's some little thing has slipped me, and I can't get back.'

"That, you know, rather bowled me over. He looked at me in such an abject way that for the life of me I couldn't keep up quite the high hectoring vein I had adopted. 'That's queer,' I said, and as I spoke I fancied I heard someone moving about down below. 'Come into my room and tell me more about it,' I said. I didn't, of course, understand this, and I tried to take him by the arm. But, of course, you might as well have tried to take hold of a puff of smoke! I had forgotten my number, I think; anyhow, I remember going into several bedrooms – it was lucky I was the only soul in that wing – until I saw my traps. 'Here we are,' I said, and sat down in the armchair; 'sit down and tell me all about it. It seems to me you have got yourself into a jolly awkward position, old chap.'

"Well, he said he wouldn't sit down; he'd prefer to flit up and down the room if it was all the same to me. And so he did, and in a little while we were deep in a long and serious talk. And presently, you know, something of those whiskies and sodas evaporated out of me, and I began to realise just a little what a thundering rum and weird business it was that I was in. There he was, semi-transparent – the proper conventional phantom, and noiseless except for his ghost of a voice – flitting to and fro in that nice, clean, chintz-hung old bedroom. You could see the gleam of the copper candlesticks through him, and the lights on the brass fender, and the corners of the framed engravings on the wall, and there he was telling me all about this wretched little life of his that had recently ended on earth. He hadn't a particularly honest face, you know, but being transparent, of course, he couldn't avoid telling the truth."

"Eh?" said Wish, suddenly sitting up in his chair.

"What?" said Clayton.

"Being transparent – couldn't avoid telling the truth – I don't see it," said Wish.

"*I* don't see it," said Clayton, with inimitable assurance. "But it *is* so, I can assure you nevertheless. I don't believe he got once a nail's breadth off the Bible truth. He told me how he had been killed – he went down into a London basement with a candle to look for a leakage of gas – and described himself as a senior English master in a London private school when that release occurred."

"Poor wretch!" said I.

"That's what I thought, and the more he talked the more I thought it. There he was, purposeless in life and purposeless out of it. He talked of his father and mother and his schoolmaster, and all who had ever been anything to him in the world, meanly. He had been too sensitive, too nervous; none of them had ever valued him properly or understood him, he said. He had never had a real friend in the world, I think; he had never had a success. He had shirked games and failed examinations. 'It's like that with some people,' he said; 'whenever I got into the examination-room or anywhere everything seemed to go.' Engaged to be married, of course – to another over-sensitive person, I suppose – when the indiscretion with the gas escape ended his affairs. 'And where are you now?' I asked. 'Not in—?'

"He wasn't clear on that point at all. The impression he gave me was of a sort of vague, intermediate state, a special reserve for souls too non-existent for anything so positive as either sin or virtue. *I* don't know. He was much too egotistical and unobservant to give me any clear idea of the kind of place, kind of country, there is on the Other Side of Things. Wherever he was, he seems to have fallen in with a set of kindred spirits: ghosts of weak Cockney young men, who were on a footing of Christian names, and among these there was certainly a lot of talk about 'going haunting' and things like that. Yes – going haunting! They seemed to think 'haunting' a tremendous adventure, and most of them funked it all the time. And so primed, you know, he had come."

"But really!" said Wish to the fire.

"These are the impressions he gave me, anyhow," said Clayton, modestly. "I may, of course, have been in a rather uncritical state, but that was the sort of background he gave to himself. He kept flitting up and down, with his thin voice going – talking, talking about his wretched self, and never a word of clear, firm statement from first to last. He was thinner and sillier and more pointless than if he had been real and alive. Only then, you know, he would not have been in my bedroom here – if he *had* been alive. I should have kicked him out."

"Of course," said Evans, "there *are* poor mortals like that."

"And there's just as much chance of their having ghosts as the rest of us," I admitted.

"What gave a sort of point to him, you know, was the fact that he did seem within limits to have found himself out. The mess he had made of haunting had depressed him terribly. He had been told it would be a 'lark': he had come expecting it to be a 'lark,' and here it was, nothing but another failure added to his record! He proclaimed himself an utter out-

and-out failure. He said, and I can quite believe it, that he had never tried to do anything all his life that he hadn't made a perfect mess of – and through all the wastes of eternity he never would. If he had had sympathy, perhaps—. He paused at that, and stood regarding me. He remarked that, strange as it might seem to me, nobody, not anyone, ever, had given him the amount of sympathy I was doing now. I could see what he wanted straight away, and I determined to head him off at once. I may be a brute, you know, but being the Only Real Friend, the recipient of the confidences of one of these egotistical weaklings, ghost or body, is beyond my physical endurance. I got up briskly. 'Don't you brood on these things too much,' I said. 'The thing you've got to do is to get out of this – get out of this sharp. You pull yourself together and *try*.' 'I can't,' he said. 'You try,' I said, and try he did."

"Try!" said Sanderson. *"How?"*

"Passes," said Clayton.

"Passes?"

"Complicated series of gestures and passes with the hands. That's how he had come in and that's how he had to get out again. Lord, what a business I had!"

"But how could *any* series of passes—" I began.

"My dear man," said Clayton, turning on me and putting a great emphasis on certain words, "you want *everything* clear. I don't know *how*. All I know is that you *do* – that *he* did, anyhow, at least. After a fearful time, you know, he got his passes right and suddenly disappeared."

"Did you," said Sanderson slowly, "observe the passes?"

"Yes," said Clayton, and seemed to think. "It was tremendously queer," he said. "There we were, I and this thin, vague ghost, in that silent room, in this silent, empty inn, in this silent little Friday-night town. Not a sound except our voices and a faint panting he made when he swung. There was the bedroom candle, and one candle on the dressing-table alight, that was all – sometimes one or other would flare up into a tall, lean, astonished flame for a space. And queer things happened. 'I can't,' he said; 'I shall never—!' And suddenly he sat down on a little chair at the foot of the bed and began to sob and sob. Lord! what a harrowing, whimpering thing he seemed!

" 'You pull yourself together,' I said, and tried to pat him on the back, and . . . my confounded hand went through him! By that time, you know, I wasn't nearly so – massive as I had been on the landing. I got the queerness of it in full. I remember snatching back my hand out of him, as it were, with a little thrill, and walking over to the dressing-table. 'You pull yourself together,' I said to him, 'and try.' And in order to encourage and help him I began to try as well."

"What!" said Sanderson, "the passes?"

"Yes, the passes."

"But—" I said, moved by an idea that eluded me for a space.

"This is interesting," said Sanderson, with his finger in his pipe-bowl. "You mean to say this ghost of yours gave way—"

"Did his level best to give away the whole confounded barrier? *Yes.*"

"He didn't," said Wish; "he couldn't. Or you'd have gone there, too."

"That's precisely it," I said, finding my elusive idea put into words for me.

"That *is* precisely it," said Clayton, with thoughtful eyes upon the fire.

For just a little while there was silence.

"And at last he did it?" said Sanderson.

"At last he did it. I had to keep him up to it hard, but he did it at last – rather suddenly. He despaired, we had a scene, and then he got up abruptly and asked me to go through the whole performance, slowly, so that he might see. 'I believe,' he said, 'if I could *see* I should spot what was wrong at once.' And he did. 'I know,' he said. 'What do you know?' said I. '*I* know,' he repeated. Then he said, peevishly, 'I *can't* do it, if you look at me – I really *can't;* it's been that, partly, all along. I'm such a nervous fellow that you put me out.' Well, we had a bit of an argument. Naturally I wanted to see; but he was as obstinate as a mule, and suddenly I had come over as tired as a dog – he tired me out. 'All right,' I said, 'I won't look at you,' and turned towards the mirror, on the wardrobe, by the bed.

"He started off very fast. I tried to follow him by looking in the looking-glass, to see just what it was had hung. Round went his arms and his hands, so, and so, and so, and then with a rush came to the last gesture of all – you stand erect and open out your arms – and so, don't you know, he stood. And then he didn't! He didn't! He wasn't! I wheeled round from the looking-glass to him. There was nothing! I was alone, with the flaring candles and a staggering mind. What had happened? Had anything happened? Had I been dreaming? . . . And then, with an absurd note of finality about it, the clock upon the landing discovered the moment was ripe for striking *one*. So! – Ping! And I was as grave and sober as a judge, with all my champagne and whisky gone into the vast serene. Feeling queer, you know – confoundedly *queer!* Queer! Good Lord!"

He regarded his cigar-ash for a moment. "That's all that happened," he said.

"And then you went to bed?" asked Evans.

"What else was there to do?"

I looked Wish in the eye. We wanted to scoff, and there was something, something perhaps in Clayton's voice and manner, that hampered our desire.

"And about these passes?" said Sanderson.

"I believe I could do them now."

"Oh!" said Sanderson, and produced a pen-knife and set himself to grub the dottel out of the bowl of his clay.

"Why don't you do them now?" said Sanderson, shutting his pen-knife with a click.

"That's what I'm going to do," said Clayton.

"They won't work," said Evans.

"If they do—" I suggested.

"You know, I'd rather you didn't," said Wish, stretching out his legs.

"Why?" asked Evans.

"I'd rather he didn't," said Wish.

"But he hasn't got 'em right," said Sanderson, plugging too much tobacco into his pipe.

"All the same, I'd rather he didn't," said Wish.

We argued with Wish. He said that for Clayton to go through those gestures was like mocking a serious matter. "But you don't believe—?" I said. Wish glanced at Clayton, who was staring into the fire, weighing something in his mind. "I do – more than half, anyhow, I do," said Wish.

"Clayton," said I, "you're too good a liar for us. Most of it was all right. But that disappearance . . . happened to be convincing. Tell us, it's a tale of cock and bull."

He stood up without heeding me, took the middle of the hearthrug, and faced me. For a moment he regarded his feet thoughtfully, and then for all the rest of the time his eyes were on the opposite wall, with an intent expression. He raised his two hands slowly to the level of his eyes and so began. . . .

Now, Sanderson is a Freemason, a member of the lodge of the Four Kings, which devotes itself so ably to the study and elucidation of all the mysteries of Masonry past and present, and among the students of this lodge Sanderson is by no means the least. He followed Clayton's motions with a singular interest in his reddish eye. "That's not bad," he said, when it was done. "You really do, you know, put things together, Clayton, in a most amazing fashion. But there's one little detail out."

"I know," said Clayton. "I believe I could tell you which."

"Well?"

"This," said Clayton, and did a queer little twist and writhing and thrust of the hands.

"Yes."

"That, you know, was what *he* couldn't get right," said Clayton. "But how do *you*—?"

"Most of this business, and particularly how you invented it, I don't understand at all," said Sanderson, "but just that phase – I do." He reflected. "These happen to be a series of gestures – connected with a certain branch of esoteric Masonry. Probably you know. Or else—*How?*" He reflected still further. "I do not see I can do any harm in telling you just the proper twist. After all, if you know, you know; if you don't, you don't."

"I know nothing," said Clayton, "except what the poor devil let out last night."

"Well, anyhow," said Sanderson, and placed his churchwarden very carefully upon the shelf over the fireplace. Then very rapidly he gesticulated with his hands.

"So?" said Clayton, repeating.

"So," said Sanderson, and took his pipe in hand again.

"Ah, *now*," said Clayton, "I can do the whole thing – right." He stood up before the waning fire and smiled at us all. But I think there was just a little hesitation in his smile. "If I begin—" he said.

"I wouldn't begin," said Wish.

"It's all right!" said Evans. "Matter is indestructible. You don't think any jiggery-pokery of this sort is going to snatch Clayton into the world of shades. Not it! You may try, Clayton, so far as I'm concerned, until your arms drop off at the wrists."

"I don't believe that," said Wish, and stood up and put his arm on Clayton's shoulder. "You've made me half-believe in that story somehow, and I don't want to see the thing done."

"Goodness!" said I, "here's Wish frightened!"

"I am," said Wish, with real or admirably feigned intensity. "I believe that if he goes through these motions right he'll *go.*"

"He'll not do anything of the sort," I cried. "There's only one way out of this world for men, and Clayton is thirty years from that. Besides . . . And such a ghost! Do you think—?"

Wish interrupted me by moving. He walked out from among our chairs and stopped beside the table and stood there. "Clayton," he said, "you're a fool."

Clayton, with a humorous light in his eyes, smiled back to him. "Wish," he said, "is right and all you others are wrong. I shall go. I shall get to the end of these passes, and as the last swish whistles through the air, Presto! – this hearthrug will be vacant, the room will be blank amazement, and a respectably dressed gentleman of fifteen stone will plump into the world of shades. I'm certain. So will you be. I decline to argue further. Let the thing be tried."

"No," said Wish, and made a step and ceased, and Clayton raised his hands once more to repeat the spirit's passing.

By that time, you know, we were all in a state of tension – largely because of the behaviour of Wish. We sat all of us with our eyes on Clayton – I, at least, with a sort of tight, stiff feeling about me as though from the back of my skull to the middle of my thighs my body had been changed to steel. And there, with a gravity that was imperturbably serene, Clayton bowed and swayed and waved his hands and arms before us. As he drew towards the end one piled up, one tingled in one's teeth. The last gesture, I have said, was to swing the arms out wide open, with the face held up. And when at last he swung out to this closing gesture I ceased even to breathe. It was ridiculous, of course, but you know that ghost-story feeling. It was after dinner, in a queer old shadowy house. Would he, after all—?

There he stood for one stupendous moment, with his arms open and his upturned face, assured and bright, in the glare of the hanging lamp. We hung through that moment as if it were an age, and then came from all of us something that was half a sigh of infinite relief and half a reassuring *"No!"* For visibly – he wasn't going. It was all nonsense. He had told an idle story, and carried it almost to conviction, that was all! . . . And then in that moment the face of Clayton changed.

It changed. It changed as a lit house changes when its lights are suddenly extinguished. His eyes were suddenly eyes that were fixed, his smile was frozen on his lips, and he stood there still. He stood there, very gently swaying.

That moment, too, was an age. And then, you know, chairs

were scraping, things were falling, and we were all moving. His knees seemed to give, and he fell forward, and Evans rose and caught him in his arms. . . .

It stunned us all. For a minute I suppose no one said a coherent thing. We believed it, yet could not believe it. . . . I came out of a muddled stupefaction to find myself kneeling beside him, and his vest and shirt were torn open, and Sanderson's hand lay on his heart. . . .

Well – the simple fact before us could very well wait our convenience; there was no hurry for us to comprehend. It lay there for an hour; it lies athwart my memory, black and amazing still, to this day. Clayton had, indeed, passed into the world that lies so near to and so far from our own, and he had gone thither by the only road that mortal man may take. But whether he did indeed pass there by that poor ghost's incantation, or whether he was stricken suddenly by apoplexy in the midst of an idle tale – as the coroner's jury would have us believe – is no matter for my judging; it is just one of those inexplicable riddles that must remain unsolved until the final solution of all things shall come. All I certainly know is that, in the very moment, in the very instant, of concluding those passes, he changed, and staggered, and fell down before us – dead!

THE PRESENCE BY THE FIRE

It never occurred to Reid that his wife lay dying until the last day of her illness. He was a man of healthy disposition, averse on principle to painful thoughts, and I doubt if in the whole of his married life his mind had dwelt for five minutes on the possibility of losing her.

They were both young, and very intimate companions – such companions as many desire to be and few become. Perhaps it was her sense of the value of this rare companionship that had made her, when first her health declined, run many an avoidable risk rather than leave him to go his way alone. He was sorry that she was ill, sorry she should suffer, and he missed her, as she lay upstairs, in a thousand ways; but though the doctor was careful to use all the "preparatory" phrases of his profession, and though her sister spoke, as she conceived, quite plainly, it was as hard for him to understand that this was more than a temporary interruption of their life, as it would have been to believe that the sun would not rise again.

The day before she died he was restless, and, after wandering about the house and taking a short walk, he occupied himself in planting out her evening primroses – a thing she had made a point of doing now for ten springs in succession. The garden she had always tended, he said, should not seem neglected when she came down again. He would rather that his own work get in arrears than that should happen.

The first realization when at last the doctor, finding all conventional euphemisms useless, told him the fact in stark, plain words, stunned him. Even then it is doubtful if he believed. He said not a word in answer, but the colour left his face, and the lines about his mouth hardened. And he walked softly, and with white, expressionless features, into her room.

He stood in the doorway and stared for a minute at her thin little features, with the eyes closed and two little lines between the brows; then went and knelt by the bed and looked closely into her face. She did not move until he touched her hair and very softly whispered her name.

Then her eyes opened for a moment, and he saw that she knew him. Her lips moved, and it seemed that she whispered one of those foolish, tender little names that happy married folk delight in inventing for one another; then she gathered her strength as if with an effort to speak distinctly. He bent mechanically, and heard the last syllable of "Au revoir."

For a moment he did not clearly understand what the words were. That was all she said, and as for him he answered not a word. He put his hand in hers, and she pressed it faintly, and then more faintly. He kissed her forehead with dry lips, and the little lines of pain faded slowly into peace.

For an hour they let him kneel, until the end came; all that time he never stirred. Then they had to tap his shoulder to rouse him from his rigour. He got up slowly, bent over her for a moment, and allowed them to lead him away.

That was how Reid parted from his wife, and for days after he behaved as a man who had been suddenly deprived of all initiative. He did no work; he went nowhere outside the house; he ate, drank and slept mechanically; and he did not even seem to suffer actively. For the most part he sat stupidly at his desk, or wandered about his big garden, looking with dull eyes at the little green buds that were now swiftly opening all about him. Not a soul ventured to speak to him of his loss; those who did not know him might have judged his mood one of absolute apathy.

But nearly a week after the funeral the floodgates of his sorrow were opened. Quite suddenly the thing came upon him. Her sister heard, him walk into the study and throw himself into a chair. Everything was still for a space, and then he sprang up again, and she heard him wailing, "Mary! Mary!" And then he ran sobbing violently and stumbling along the passage to his room. It was grotesquely like a little child that had suddenly been hurt.

He locked his door! And her sister, fearing what might

happen, went along the passage. She thought of rapping at the door, but on second thoughts she refrained. After listening awhile she went away.

It was long after the first violence of his grief had passed that Reid first spoke of his feelings. He who had been a matter-of-fact materialist was converted, I found, to a belief in immortality by the pitiless logic of her uncompleted life. But I think it was an imperfect, doubting belief even at the best. And to strengthen it, perhaps, he began to show a growing interest in the inquiries of those who are sifting whatever evidence there may be of the return of those who are dead.

"For I want my wife now," said he. "I want her in this life, I want her about me – her comfort, her presence. What does it matter that I shall meet her again when I am changed, and she is changed? It was the dear trivialities, the little moments, the touch of her hand, the sound of her voice in the room with me, her distant singing in the garden, and her footfall on the stairs. If I could believe that," he said, "if I could believe . . ."

In that spirit it was that he kept to the old home, and would scarcely hear that a thing within or without should be altered in any way. The white curtains that had been there the last autumn hung dirty in the windows, and the little desk that had been her own in the study stood there still, with the pen thrown down as he fancied she had left it.

"Here, if anywhere," he said, "she is at home. Here, if anywhere, her presence lives."

Her sister left him when a housekeeper was obtained, and he went on living alone, working little and communicating for the most part with these dead memories. He loved nothing so much as to talk of her, and I think that in those days I was of service to him. He would take me about the house, pointing to this trivial thing and that, and telling me some little act of hers, some freak or some witticism with which he associated it. And he always spoke of her as of one who still lived.

"She does," so-and-so, he would say; "she likes" so-and-so. We would pace up and down the rich lawn of his house. "My wife is particularly fond of those big white lilies," he would say, "and this year they are finer than ever." So the summer passed and the autumn came.

And one day late in the evening he came to me, walking round the house and tapping at the French window of my study, and as he came in out of the night I noticed how deadly white and sunken his face was, and how bright his eyes.

"I have seen her," he said to me in a low, clear voice. "She has visited me. I knew she was watching me and near me. I have felt her presence for weeks and weeks. And now she had come."

He was intensely excited, and it was some time before I could get any clear story from him.

He had been sitting by the fire in his study, musing, no doubt going over for the hundredth time, day by day and almost hour by hour, as he was wont to do, one of the summer holidays they had spent together. He was staring, he said, into the glowing coals, and almost imperceptibly then there grew upon him the impression that he was not alone. The thought took shape slowly in his mind, but with a strange quality of absolute conviction that she was sitting in the armchair in front of him, as she had done so often in the old days, and watching him a-dreaming. For a moment he did not dare to look up, lest he should find this a mere delusion.

Then slowly he raised his eyes. He was dimly aware of footsteps advancing along the passage as he did so. A wave of bitter disappointment swept over him as he saw the chair was empty, and this incontinently gave place to a tumult of surprise and joyful emotion. For he saw her – saw her distinctly. She was standing behind the chair, leaning over the back of it, and smiling the tender smile he knew so well. So in her life she had stood many a time and listened to him, smiling gently. The firelight played upon her face.

"I saw her as plainly as I see you," he said. "I saw the smile in her eyes, and my heart leapt out to her."

For a moment he was motionless, entranced, and with an instantaneous appreciation of the transitoriness of this appearance. Then suddenly the door opened, the shadows in the room rushed headlong, and the housemaid came in with his lamp lit and without a shade – a dazzling glare of naked flame. The yellow light splashed over the room, and brought out everything clear and vivid.

By mere reflex action he turned his head at the sound of the door-handle and forthwith turned it back again. But the face he had longed for so patiently had vanished with the shadows, before the light. Everything was abruptly plain and material. The girl replenished the fire, moved the armchair on one side, and took away the scuttle lining to refill it with coals. A curious bashfulness made Reid pretend to make notes at his table until these offices were accomplished.

Then he looked across the fireplace again, and the room was empty. The sense of her presence, too, had gone. He called upon her name again and again, rubbed his eyes, and tried to force her return by concentrating his mind upon her. But nothing availed. He could see her no more.

He allowed me to cross-examine him in the most detailed way upon this story. His manner was so sane, so convincing, and his honesty so indisputable, that I went to bed that night with my beliefs and disbeliefs greatly shaken. Hitherto I had doubted every ghost story I had heard; but here at last was one of a different quality. Indeed, I went to bed that night an unwilling convert to the belief in phantasms of those who are dead, and all that that belief implies.

My faith in Reid was confirmed by the fact that from late August, when this happened, until December, he did not see the apparition again. Had it been an hallucination begotten of his own intense brooding, it must inevitably have recurred. But it was presently to be proved beyond all question that the thing he saw was an exterior presence. Night after night he sat in his study, longing for the repetition of that strange experience; and at last, after many nights, he saw her for the second time.

It was earlier in the evening, but with the shorter winter days the room was already dark. Once more he looked into his study fire, and once more that fire glowed redly. Then there came the same sense of her presence, the same hesitation before he raised his eyes. But this time he looked over the chair at once, and saw her without any flash of disappointment.

At the instant he felt not the faintest suspicion that his senses had deceived him. For a moment he was dumb. He was seized with an intense longing to touch her hand. Then came into his head some half-forgotten story that one must speak first to a spirit. He leant forward.

"*Mary*!" he said very softly. But she neither moved nor spoke. And then suddenly it seemed that she grew less distinct.

"*Mary*!" he whispered, with a sudden pang of doubt. Her features grew unfamiliar.

Then suddenly he rose to his feet, and as he did so the making of the illusion was demonstrated. The high light on a vase that had been her cheek moved to the right; the shadow that had been her arm moved to the left.

Few people realize how little we actually see of what is before our eyes; a patch of light, a patch of shadow, and all the rest our memory and our imagination supply. A chance grouping of dim forms in the dusky firelit study had furnished all the suggestion his longing senses had required. His eyes and his heart and the humour of chance had cheated him.

He stood staring. For a moment the disintegration of the figure filled him with a sense of grotesque horror and dismay. For a moment it seemed beyond the sanity of things. Then, as he realized the deception his senses had contrived, he sat down again, put his elbows on the table, and buried his face in his hands.

About ten he came and told me. He told me in a clear, hard voice, without a touch of emotion, recording a remarkable fact. "As I told you the other thing, it is only right that I should tell you this," he said. Then he sat silently for a space.

"She will come no more," he said at last. "She will come no more." And suddenly he rose, and without a greeting passed out into the night.

THE INVASION FROM MARS

1 A FALLING STAR

The first star was seen early in the morning rushing over Winchester eastward, high in the atmosphere. Hundreds must have seen it, and taken it for an ordinary falling star. For in those days no one gave a thought to the outer worlds of space as sources of human danger. At most, terrestrial men fancied there might be other men upon Mars, perhaps inferior to themselves and ready to welcome a missionary enterprise. Yet across the gulf of space, minds that are to our minds as ours are to the beasts that perish, intellects vast and cool and unsympathetic, regarded this earth with envious eyes, and slowly and surely drew their plans against us.

No one seems to have troubled to look for the fallen thing that night. But early in the morning it was found, almost entirely buried in the sand, among the scattered splinters of a fir-tree on the common between Horsell, Woking, and Ottershaw. The uncovered part had the appearance of a huge cylinder, caked over, and its outline softened, by a thick, scaly, dun-coloured incrustation. It had a diameter of about thirty yards. A stirring noise within the cylinder was ascribed at first to the unequal cooling of its surface, for at that time it did not occur to anyone that it might be hollow.

When, about sunset, I joined the crowd at the edge of the pit the thing had dug by its impact with the soil, the end of the cylinder was being screwed out from within. Nearly two feet of shining screw projected. Somebody blundered against me, and I narrowly missed being pitched on the top of the screw. As I turned to avoid the fall the lid of the cylinder fell upon the gravel with a ringing concussion. For a moment the cavity seemed perfectly black, for I had the sunset in my eyes.

I think everyone expected to see a man emerge – possibly something a little unlike us terrestrial men, but in all essentials a man. I know I did. But, looking, I presently saw something stirring within the shadow – greyish, billowy movements, one above another, and then two luminous discs like eyes. Then something resembling a little grey snake, about the thickness of a walking stick coiled up out of the writhing middle, and wriggled in the air towards me, and then another.

A big, greyish, rounded bulk, the size, perhaps, of a bear, was rising slowly and painfully out of the cylinder. As it bulged up and caught the light, it glistened like wet leather. Two large, dark-coloured eyes were regarding me steadfastly. It was rounded, and had, one might say, a face. There was a mouth under the eyes, the lipless brim of which quivered and panted, and dropped saliva. The body heaved and pulsated convulsively. A lank, tentacular appendage gripped the edge of the cylinder, another swayed in the air.

Those who have never seen a living Martian can scarcely imagine the strange horror of their appearance. The peculiar V-shaped mouth with its pointed upper lip, the absence of brow ridges, the absence of a chin beneath the wedge-like lower lip, the incessant quivering of this mouth, the Gorgon groups of tentacles, the tumultuous breathing of the lungs in a strange atmosphere, the evident heaviness and painfulness of movement, due to the greater gravitational energy of the earth – above all, the extraordinary intensity of the immense eyes – culminated in an effect akin to nausea. There was something fungoid in the oily brown skin, something in the clumsy deliberation of their tedious movements unspeakably terrible. Even at this first encounter, this first glimpse, I was overcome with disgust and dread.

Suddenly the monster vanished. It had toppled over the brim of the cylinder, and fallen into the pit with a thud like the fall of a great mass of leather. I heard it give a peculiar thick cry, and forthwith another of these creatures appeared darkly in the deep shadow of the aperture.

At that my rigour of terror passed away. I turned, and, running madly, made for the first group of trees, perhaps a hundred yards away; but I ran slantingly and stumbling, for I could not avert my face from these things. There, among some young pine trees and furze bushes, I stopped, panting, and waited further developments. Once a leash of thin black whips, like the arms of an octopus, flashed across the sunset, and was immediately withdrawn, and afterwards a thin rod rose up, joint by joint, bearing at its apex a circular disc that spun with a wobbling motion.

Suddenly there was a flash of light, and a quantity of luminous greenish smoke came out of the pit in three distinct puffs, which drove up, one after the other, straight into the still air. At the same time a faint hissing sound became audible. Beyond the pit stood a little wedge of people, a little knot of small vertical black shapes upon the black ground. As the green smoke rose their faces flashed out pallid green, and faded again as it vanished.

Then slowly the hissing passed into humming, into a long, loud droning noise. Slowly a humped shape rose out of the pit, and the ghost of a beam of light seemed to flicker out from it. Forthwith, flashes of actual flame, a bright glare leaping from one to another, sprang from the scattered group of men. It was as if some invisible jet impinged upon them and flashed into white flame. It was as if each man were suddenly and momentarily turned to fire.

Then, by the light of their own destruction, I saw them

staggering and falling, and their supporters turning to run.

I stood staring, not as yet realizing that this was death leaping from man to man in that little distant crowd. All I felt was that it was something strange. An almost noiseless and blinding flash of light, and a man fell headlong and lay still, and as the unseen shaft of heat passed over them, pine trees burst into fire, and every dry furze-bush became with one dull thud a mass of flames. It is still a matter of wonder how the Martians are able to slay men so swiftly and so silently. Many think that in some way they are able to generate an intense heat in a chamber of practically absolute non-conductivity. This intense heat they project in a parallel beam against any object they choose by means of a polished parabolic mirror of unknown composition – much as the parabolic mirror of a lighthouse projects a beam of light. But no one has absolutely proved these details. However it was done, it is certain that a beam of heat is the essence of the matter – heat, and invisible, instead of visible, light. Whatever is combustible flashes into flame at its touch, lead runs like water, it softens iron, cracks and melts glass, and when it falls upon water incontinently that explodes into steam.

That night nearly forty people lay under the starlight about the pit, charred and distorted beyond recognition, and all night long the common from Horsell to Maybury was deserted, and brightly ablaze.

II FIGHTING BEGINS

It was in a storm that I first saw the Martians at large, on the night of the third falling star. How can I describe the thing I saw? A monstrous tripod, higher than many houses, striding over the young pine trees, and smashing them aside in its career; a walking engine of glittering metal, striding now across the heather, articulate ropes of steel dangling from it, and the clattering tumult of its passage mingling with the riot of the thunder. A flash, and it came out vividly, heeling over one way with two feet in the air, to vanish, and reappear almost instantly, as it seemed, with the next flash, a hundred yards nearer. Can you imagine a milking-stool tilted and bowled violently along the ground? That was the impression those instant flashes gave. But instead of a milking-stool, imagine it a great body of machinery on a tripod stand.

Seen nearer, the thing was incredibly strange, for it was no mere insensate machine driving on its way. Machine it was, with a ringing metallic pace, and long flexible glittering tentacles (one of which gripped a young pine tree) swinging and rattling about its strange body. It picked its road as it went striding along, and the brazen hood that surmounted it moved to and fro with the inevitable suggestion of a head looking about it. Behind the main body was a huge thing of white metal like a gigantic fisherman's basket, and puffs of green smoke squirted out from the joints of the limbs as the monster swept by me.

All that night the creatures were busy – communicating, I suppose, and maturing their plans. It was not until the next morning that our resistance began. The fighting I saw took place at Shepperton Wey, where a crowd of fugitives were waiting their turn to cross the river by the ferry.

Suddenly we saw a rush of smoke far away up the river, a puff of smoke that jerked up into the air, and hung; and forthwith the ground heaved under foot, and a heavy explosion shook the air, smashing two or three windows in the houses near, and leaving us astonished.

Quickly, one after the other, one, two, three, four of the armoured Martians appeared, far away over the little trees, across the flat meadows that stretch towards Chertsey, and striding hurriedly towards the river. Little cowled figures they seemed at first, going with a rolling motion and as fast as flying birds.

Then, advancing obliquely towards us, came a fifth. Their armoured bodies glittered in the sun as they swept swiftly forward upon the guns, growing rapidly larger as they drew nearer. One on the extreme left – the remotest, that is – flourished a huge case high in the air, and the ghostly terrible heat-ray I had already seen on Friday night smote towards Chertsey, and struck the town.

'Get under water!' I shouted, unheeded. And, as the first Martian towered over head scarcely a couple of hundred feet away, I flung myself under the surface.

When I raised my head, it was on the bank, and, in a stride, wading halfway across. The knees of its foremost legs bent at the further bank, and in another moment it had raised itself to its full height again, close to the village of Shepperton. Forthwith the six guns, which, unknown to anyone on the right bank, had been hidden behind the outskirts of that village, fired simultaneously. The sudden near concussions, the last close upon the first, made my heart jump. The monster was already raising the case generating the heat-ray as the first shell burst six yards above the hood.

Simultaneously two other shells burst in the air near the body as the hood twisted round in time to receive, but not in time to dodge, the fourth shell.

The shell burst clean in the face of the thing. The hood bulged, flashed, was whirled off in a dozen tattered fragments of red flesh and glittering metal.

'Hit!' shouted I, with something between a scream and

a cheer.

I heard answering shouts from the people in the water about me. I could have leapt out of the water with that momentary exultation.

The decapitated colossus reeled like a drunken giant, but it did not fall over. It recovered its balance by a miracle, and, no longer heeding its steps, and with the camera that fired the heat-ray now rigidly upheld, it reeled swiftly upon Shepperton. The living intelligence, the Martian within the hood, was slain and splashed to the four winds of heaven, and the thing was now but a mere intricate device of metal whirling to destruction. It drove along in a straight line, incapable of guidance. It struck the tower of Shepperton church, smashing it down as the impact of a battering-ram might have done, swerved aside, blundered on, and collapsed with a tremendous impact into the river out of my sight.

A violent explosion shook the air, and a spout of water, steam, mud, and shattered metal shot far up into the sky. As the camera of the heat-ray hit the water, the latter had incontinently flashed into steam. In another moment a huge wave, like a muddy tidal bore, but almost scalding hot, came sweeping round the bend upstream. I saw people struggling shorewards, and heard their screaming faintly above the seething and roar of the Martian's collapse.

Then again I ducked, for the other Martians were

advancing. When for a moment I raised my head to take breath and throw the water from my eyes, the steam was rising in a whirling white fog that at first hid the Martians altogether. The noise was deafening. Then I saw them dimly, colossal figures of grey, magnified by the mist. They had passed by me, and two were stooping over the tumultuous ruins of their comrade.

The third and fourth stood beside him in the water, one perhaps two hundred yards from me, the other towards Laleham. The generators of the heat-rays waved high, and the hissing beams smote down this way and that.

The air was full of sound, a deafening and confusing conflict of noises, the clangorous din of the Martians, the crash of falling houses, the thud of trees, fences, sheds, flashing into flame, and the crackling and roaring of fire. Dense black smoke was leaping up to mingle with the steam from the river, and as the heat-ray went to and fro over Weybridge, its impact was marked by flashes of incandescent white, that gave place at once to a smoky dance of lurid flames.

For a moment, perhaps, I stood there, breast-high in the almost boiling water, dumbfounded at my position, hopeless of escape. Through the reek I could see the people who had been with me in the river scrambling out of the water through the reeds, like little frogs hurrying through grass from the advance of a man, or running to and fro in utter dismay on the towing-path.

Then suddenly the white flashes of the heat-ray came leaping towards me. The houses caved in as they dissolved at its touch, and darted out flames; the trees changed to fire with a roar. It flickered up and down the towing-path, licking off the people who ran this way and that, and came down to the water's edge not fifty yards from where I stood. It swept across the river to Shepperton, and the water in its track rose in a boiling wheal crested with steam. I turned shoreward.

In another moment the huge wave, well-nigh at the boiling-point, had rushed upon me. I screamed aloud, and, scalded, half-blinded, agonized, I staggered through the leaping, hissing water towards the shore. Had my feet stumbled, it would have been the end. I fell helplessly, in full sight of the Martians, upon the broad, bare gravelly spit that runs down to mark the angle of the Wey and Thames. I expected nothing but death. I have a dim memory of the foot of a Martian coming down within a score of feet of my head, driving straight into the loose gravel, whirling it this way and that, and lifting again; of a long suspense, and then of the four carrying the *débris* of their comrade between them, now clear, and then presently faint, through a veil of smoke, receding interminably, as it seemed to me, across a vast space of river and meadow. And then, very slowly, I realized that by a miracle I had escaped.

But it was not on the heat-ray that the Martians chiefly relied in their march on London. The monsters I saw that evening as I fled were armed with tubes which they discharged like guns. There was no flash, no smoke, simply that loaded detonation. Every minute I expected the fire of some hidden battery to spring upon them, but the evening calm was unbroken. Their figures grew smaller as they receded, and presently the gathering night had swallowed them up. Only towards Sunbury was a dark appearance, as though a conical hill had suddenly come into being there, and remoter across the river, towards Walton, I saw another such summit. They grew lower and broader even as I stared. These, as I knew later, were the black smoke. It was heavy, this vapour, heavier than the densest smoke, so that, after the first tumultuous uprush and outflow of its impact, it sank down through the air and poured over the ground in a manner rather liquid than gaseous, abandoning the hills, and streaming into the valleys and ditches and watercourses, even as I have heard the carbonic acid gas that pours from volcanic clefts is wont to do. And the touch of that vapour, the inhaling of its pungent wisps, was death to all that breathes.

One has to imagine the fate of those batteries towards Esher, waiting so tensely in the twilight, as well as one may. Survivors there were none. One may picture the orderly expectation, the officers alert and watchful, the gunners ready, the ammunition piled to hand, the limber gunners with their horses and wagons, the groups of civilian spectators standing as near as they were permitted, the evening stillness, the ambulances and hospital tents, with the burnt and wounded from Weybridge; then the dull resonance of the shots the Martians fired, and the clumsy projectile whirling over the trees and houses, and smashing amidst the neighbouring fields.

One may picture, too, the sudden shifting of the attention, the swiftly spreading coils and bellyings of that blackness advancing headlong, towering heavenward, turning the twilight to a palpable darkness, a strange and horrible antagonist of vapour striding upon its victims, men and horses near it seen dimly running, shrieking, falling headlong, shouts of dismay, the guns suddenly abandoned, men choking and writhing on the ground, and the swift broadening out of the opaque cone of smoke. And then, night and extinction – nothing but a silent mass of impenetrable vapour hiding its dead.

III DEAD LONDON

So you understand the roaring wave of fear that swept through the greatest city in the world just as Monday was dawning – the stream of flight rising swiftly to a torrent, lashing in a foaming tumult round the railway stations, banked up into a horrible struggle about the shipping in the Thames, and hurrying by every available channel northward and eastward. By ten o'clock the police organization, and by midday even the railway organizations, were losing coherency, losing shape and efficiency, guttering, softening, running at last in that swift liquefaction of the social body.

All the railway lines north of the Thames and the South-Eastern people at Cannon Street had been warned by midnight on Sunday, and trains were being filled, people were fighting savagely for standing-room in the carriages, even at two o'clock. By three people were being trampled and crushed even in Bishopsgate Street; a couple of hundred yards or more from Liverpool Street station revolvers were fired, people stabbed, and the policemen who had been sent to direct the traffic, exhausted and infuriated, were breaking the heads of the people they were called out to protect.

And as the day advanced the engine-drivers and stokers refused to return to London, the pressure of the flight drove the people in an ever-thickening multitude away from the stations and along the northward-running roads. By midday a Martian had been seen at Barnes, and a cloud of slowly sinking black vapour drove along the Thames and across the flats of Lambeth, cutting off all escape over the bridges in its advance.

If one could have hung that June morning in a balloon in the blazing blue above London, every northward and eastward road running out of the infinite tangle of streets would have seemed stippled black with the streaming fugitives, each dot a human agony of terror and physical distress.

Directly below him the balloonist would have seen the network of streets far and wide, houses, churches, squares, crescents, gardens – already derelict – spread out like a huge map, and in the southward *blotted*. Over Ealing, Richmond, Wimbledon, it would have seemed as if some monstrous pen had flung ink upon the chart. Steadily, incessantly, each black splash grew and spread, shooting out ramifications this way and that, now banking itself against rising ground, now pouring swiftly over a crest into a new-found valley, exactly as a gout of ink would spread itself upon blotting-paper.

And beyond, over the blue hills that rise southward of the river, the glittering Martians went to and fro, calmly and methodically spreading their poison-cloud over this patch of country, and then over that, laying it again with their steam-jets when it had served its purpose, and taking possession of the conquered country. They do not seem to have aimed at extermination so much as at complete demoralization and the destruction of any opposition. They exploded any stores of powder they came upon, cut every telegraph, and wrecked the railways here and there. They were hamstringing mankind. They seemed in no hurry to extend the field of operations, and they did not come beyond the central part of London all that day. It is possible that a very considerable number of people in London stuck to their houses through Monday morning. Certain it is that many died at home, suffocated by the black smoke.

I have not space here to tell you of my adventures during the days that followed – of how I saw men caught for the Martians' food, of how the third falling star smashed the house where I was resting, and of what I saw while I was hiding there. When I came out into the air again I found about me the landscape, weird and lurid, of another planet. Everywhere spread the red weed, whose seed the Martians had brought with them. All round were red cactus-shaped plants, knee-high, without a solitary terrestrial growth to dispute their footing. The trees near me were dead and brown, but further, a network of red threads scaled the still living stems. I went on my way to Hampstead through scarlet and crimson trees; it was like walking through an avenue of gigantic blood-drops.

IV HOW THE MARTIANS WERE SLAIN

It was near South Kensington that I first heard the howling. It crept almost imperceptibly upon my senses. It was a sobbing alternation of two notes, 'Ulla, ulla, ulla, ulla,' keeping on perpetually. I stopped, wondering at this strange, remote wailing. It was as if that mighty desert of houses had found a voice for its fear and solitude. It was not until I emerged from Baker Street that I saw, far away over the trees in the clearness of the sunset, the hood of the Martian giant from which this howling proceeded. I watched him for some time, but he did not move.

I came upon the wrecked handling machine halfway to St John's Wood Station. At first I thought a house had fallen across the road. It was only as I clambered among the ruins that I saw, with a start, this mechanical Samson lying, with its tentacles bent and smashed and twisted, among the ruins it had made. The fore part was shattered. It seemed as if it had driven blindly straight at the house, and had been overwhelmed in its overthrow.

A little beyond the ruins about the smashed handling machine I came upon the red weed again, and found Regent's Canal a spongy mass of dark red vegetation.

The dusky houses about me stood faint and tall and dim;

the trees towards the park were growing black. All about me the red weed clambered among the ruins, writhing to get above me in the dim. Night, the mother of fear and mystery, was coming upon me. London gazed at me spectrally. The windows in the white houses were like the eye-sockets of skulls. About me my imagination found a thousand noiseless enemies moving. Terror seized me, a horror of my temerity. Far away, I saw a second Martian, motionless as the first, standing in the park towards the Zoological Gardens, and silent.

An insane resolve possessed me. I would die and end it. And I would save myself even the trouble of killing myself. I marched on recklessly towards this Titan, and then, as I drew nearer and the light grew, I saw that a multitude of black birds was circling and clustering about the hood. At that my heart gave a bound, and I began running along the road. Great mounds had been heaped about the crest of the hill, making a huge redoubt of it. It was the final and largest place the Martians made. And from behind these heaps there rose a thin smoke against the sky. Against the skyline an eager dog ran and disappeared. The thought that had flashed into my mind grew real, grew credible. I felt no fear, only a wild, trembling exultation, as I ran up the hill towards the motionless monster. Out of the hood hung lank shreds of brown at which the hungry birds pecked and tore.

In another moment I had scrambled up the earthen rampart and stood upon its crest, and the interior of the redoubt was below me. A mighty space it was, with gigantic machines here and there within it, huge mounds of material and strange shelter places. And, scattered about it, some in their overturned war-machines, some in the now rigid handling machines, and a dozen of them stark and silent and laid in a row, were the Martians – *dead!* – slain by the putrefactive and disease bacteria against which their systems were unprepared; slain as the red weed was being slain; slain, after all man's devices had failed, by the humblest things that God, in His wisdom, had put upon this earth.

Already when I watched them they were irrevocably doomed, dying and rotting even as they went to and fro. It was inevitable. By the toll of a billion deaths man has bought his birthright of the earth, and it is his against all comers; it would still be his were the Martians ten times as mighty as they are. For neither do men live nor die in vain.

www.ingramcontent.com/pod-product-compliance
Lightning Source LLC
Chambersburg PA
CBHW060403030726
47497CB00003B/833
9781447406648